LIVING THE GIMMICK

BOBBY MATHEWS

ADVANCED PRAISE
LIVING THE GIMMICK
BY BOBBY MATHEWS

"At times a wild and surreal trip through the subculture of old school pro wrestling and at other times a deft love letter to the passions that drive us all, *LIVING THE GIMMICK* is a rollicking good time. Bobby Mathews obviously loves three things: The South, pro wrestling, and a good mystery."

—**S.A. Cosby**, NY Times bestselling author of *RAZORBLADE TEARS*

"Mathews has written a glorious, noir-steeped homage to pro wrestling, all the more remarkable in its ardent fidelity. *LIVING THE GIMMICK* rocks hard."

—**Laird Barron**, author of *BLOOD STANDARD*

"*LIVING THE GIMMICK* is a bruising romp about pro wrestling, friendship, betrayal, and the lies we let ourselves believe. Bobby Mathews' career as a journalist serves him well in his debut novel; the prose is punchy, the atmosphere pungent. Mathews depicts a world of scripted violence, of showmanship and pain, where the truth is hidden behind the glam and glitter."

—**Chris Swann**, USA Today bestseller, winner of *Southern Living's Best Southern Books of 2017 Award*

"Mathews's impressive debut murder mystery is as much a gritty homage to the excessive, violent, glam rock world of professional wrestling as it is a testimony of how it's evolved from its oftentimes ruthless heyday to the glitzy entertainment machine it is now. *LIVING THE GIMMICK* is a headlock wrapped in noir sensibilities as it slams down a universal question: how much do we really know the ones we love and trust?"

—**Heather Levy**, author *WALKING THROUGH NEEDLES*

"High-class writing about hard-luck people. Timely, bold and brutal. Bobby is a writer to watch."

—**Libby Cudmore**, author of *THE BIG REWIND*

"Follow Bobby Mathews into the dank and dingy world of professional wrestling, where the punches aren't getting pulled, best friends are enemies, and murder flips the script. This is expert level storytelling where every word sets the reader up for *LIVING THE GIMMICK*'s body slam of an ending."

—**Mark Westmoreland**, author of *A VIOLENT GOSPEL*

More Praise
for LIVING THE GIMMICK

"Mathews writes in smooth, almost transparent strokes that propel the narrative along with such force, you'll read the entire novel in one sitting. The seedy world of wrestling and the badasses who populate it come alive on the page. Kayfabe? Hardly. This is as real and gritty as noir gets."
—**Hank Early**, author of *HEAVEN'S CROOKED LITTLE FINGER*

"With over twenty years in the vibrant and often insane world of professional wrestling, I can say that Bobby Mathews nails the details and treats wrestling respectfully while tantalizing you with a hell of a murder mystery in his kickass book, *LIVING THE GIMMICK*."
—**April Hunter,** pro wrestler, model, actress and writer

"Bobby Mathews understands wrestling and writing. *LIVING THE GIMMICK* is a tale which deftly weaves a gripping murder mystery full of references and nods to the days of the wrestling territories and all its greats. Fans of wrestling, crime stories, and damn good writing will all enjoy this novel."
—**Hector Acosta**, Edgar nominee and Best American Mystery Stories honoree, author of *HARDWAY*

LIVING
★★★★★ THE ★★★★★
GIMMICK

A WRESTLING NOVEL

BOBBY MATHEWS

SHOTGUN HONEY

2022

Published by **Shotgun Honey Books**

215 Loma Road
Charleston, WV 25314
www.ShotgunHoney.com
Cover by Bad Fido.

First Printing 2022.

ISBN-10: 1-956957-07-3
ISBN-13: 978-1-956957-07-5

9 8 7 6 5 4 3 2 1   22 21 20 19 18 17

This one is for my Dad, Wesley C. Mathews,
who sparked my love of pro wrestling
when I was four years old.

Thank you, Dad, for everything. I love you.

LIVING THE GIMMICK

ONE

CLOSING TIME, WHEN the lights come up, the music is silenced, and the drunks go home. The tabs get paid, the regulars shuffle out the door and weave their separate ways home. Sometimes the couples come uncoupled, recoiling in near horror at who or what they were considering taking home. Bright lights and last call are the enemies of the drunken hookup. Except when they're not.

I walked the last ones out, turned the locks closed behind them, and emptied the tip jars. Hit 'No Sale' on the cash register and changed singles out for twenties and tens. The cash went in my wallet. I closed out the day, and the register began spitting out its daily report on a long, narrow white spool of receipt paper. While it printed, I restocked the cooler. Two cases of Bud Light, a half a case of Miller and another case of Coors. Wipe down the bar with a mostly-clean damp rag and then pour the last of the coffee into a thick china mug. I put it at the end of the bar and sat down to read the tape. The tension in my shoulders eased as I read the tape. It had been a good night, for a Tuesday. Might make my nut this month. Sip dark, bitter coffee and let the after-hours silence wash over me like a gentle wave.

The banging at the door didn't startle me, exactly. Plenty of patrons leave their wallet, or their coats. I never open up after closing, though. They can reclaim their property the next day. It's all the same to me. But this knock was insistent. Whoever it was didn't plan on going away. He—it had to be a guy—would beat out 'shave and a haircut, two bits' and then alternate with long, repeated paradiddles of a song I knew but couldn't place. I waited.

He kept going for a full five minutes, and I kept getting madder about it. Finally, I dragged ass off the stool and went to the frosted, opaque door that said Donovan's Public House in gilt letters. I unlocked the door and swung it open.

Ray Wilder grinned back at me, his bleached blonde hair swept back and gelled in place, wearing a tailored suit that must've cost more than my entire liquor inventory. He was wearing a camel's hair coat, gold-rimmed glasses, and he smelled of good bay rum. He swept past me into the bar and whipped off his knee-length coat.

"It's about time," he said. "You always were a stubborn son of a bitch. Pour me a drink, would you?" He took a seat next to the end of the bar and picked up the tape I'd been examining.

"Jesus, that's depressing. You used to make that just for walking in the building."

I went to the liquor cabinet where I kept a bottle of Bushmills Black Label single-malt Irish whiskey and pulled it out, along with a pair of glasses. I put one in front of Ray and poured a generous shot. My own was a little less generous. I knew the dangers of trying to keep up with Ray Wilder.

The creases around Ray's eyes and mouth were deeper than I remembered. His hair was thinner, and his body was thicker. His face was tanned and lined from age. The scar tissue on his forehead looked like pink taffy. He was fifteen years older than me, and still in the life.

"Looking good, champ," I said. We clicked glasses, and he drained his in one gulp. I refilled it for him, and he downed the next one, too. After that, he didn't wait for me to offer the bottle. He grabbed it himself and poured dark amber liquor up to the rim. With two belts in him, he seemed a little calmer. His hands didn't shake this time when he raised the glass, and he sipped a little slower.

"You can lie to your friends, and I'll lie to mine, but let's not lie to each other," he said. "Jesus, the drive from Atlanta. You remember it?"

I did. A straight shot down I-20 out of the city and into the scrub pines of western Georgia, that feeling of flying along in the middle of nowhere with most of the exits dark and quiet after ten p.m., the bump at the Georgia-Alabama line and the sound of tires whining over grooved, rough pavement. A little more than two hours from Hartsfield International Airport to downtown Birmingham.

"You're on the southern loop this week?"

"Yeah, the pay-per-view in Atlanta was tonight. Tomorrow we're here. Then Dothan and Pensacola, finish up in Tallahassee."

I shook my head, thinking of the lonely miles in the car. Professional wrestlers spend most of their lives on the road. I'd done loops like that for twenty years, took the money I'd saved and opened a bar. Ray was still at it. He didn't wrestle anymore, but he was still out there at ringside every night, managing some kid the company thought would be the next big thing. He still took bumps, selling his ass off for the good guys. I tuned in every now and then, and he was still just as magnetic as ever. When he was on the screen, it was impossible to look away.

He was my best friend.

"It's not like you remember it," he said. "It's all politics now. Whose ass you kiss, who your friends are."

I tipped some whiskey into my coffee and swirled it around a little.

"It was always that way. You know that."

He shook his head.

"You're not there," he said. "It's worse. You can't do anything anymore. They don't want anyone to get over—they want the promotion to get over, not the performers. Do something to get yourself over, they'll take you off TV."

"You getting heat?"

"Nothing I can't handle, but I'll tell you, it changes the way the boys treat each other. We used to be on the same side. You remember that?"

"Sure," I said. What I remembered most was that you picked your battles. You found guys who were like you, guys you could work with and trust, and you looked out for each other. The rest of the locker room was on its own. But Ray didn't remember it that way. He was still on the road, still making the towns and putting on better performances than wrestlers half his age. He'd spilled more blood, wrestled more matches, and banged more women than anybody I ever knew. If he remembered things differently than me, what of it?

I was a long way and a lot of lonesome miles out of the life. Ray was still there, still running after the spotlight, still chasing the money.

"Now they got rules, I mean real rules, not like what we used to have. You know you can't blade anymore? They had a cage match tonight, nobody bled. A cage match without blood is like a kiss without a squeeze, baby. It's not like it was. We can't bleed, we can't cheat. I'll tell you, it's almost like having a real job."

"So do something else."

Ray took a look around the silent bar with its ghosts of patrons not-long departed. I knew what he was seeing. The champ was a guy who liked to party, who never let anybody else pay for his drinks, who stayed up all night just because he could. He'd been in bars all over the world. My place wasn't much different than the saloons we'd run through twenty, maybe thirty years before.

"You mean like this?" Ray said. "Sling drinks for punk kids, do all that customer service shit? Buddy, you're a better man than me."

"That was never in doubt," I said, and we both laughed. But I didn't like the way Ray's words made me feel small, as if there was something vaguely embarrassing about what I was doing. "What's wrong with it?"

He kept looking. The bar where we sat was made of oak and worn smooth by time and use, an L-shaped thing that ran nearly the entire length of the narrow building. The stools were sturdy, swivel-seated things, and the tables scattered around the room were two-tops with matching black hardback chairs. There was a small stage, little more than a platform, where undiscovered musicians played sometimes for tips and watered-down drinks. Along the far wall was a line of high-backed booths so you could feel like you had some privacy. Beyond them, a small door led to a game room with a pair of pool tables and an old pinball machine that worked almost as often as it didn't. The whole thing wasn't much, but it was mine.

"There's nothing wrong with it," Ray said after a while. He shook his head, laughed to himself. "You always wanted something like this. You own the building?"

"Yeah, got a couple apartments upstairs, too."

Ray nodded at the numbers on the tape.

"That what you make every night?"

"No," I said. "But it's pretty good for a Tuesday. Toward the weekend it picks up a good bit."

"Jesus, it'd have to."

Ray drummed his fingers on the table. I heard the tap-tap-tap of his Gucci loafers on the hardwood floor. There was something weighing on his mind. Ray was rarely nervous, and when he was, he couldn't keep it in long. I figured he'd tell me what it was eventually.

"It's good to have something. I never had anything beyond this, you know?" He didn't wait for me to respond. "Hell, I never wanted anything beyond this. I don't know, maybe my Daddy didn't love me enough, but I never got my fill of it. You come out from the curtain and the crowd goes wild. Don't you miss it?"

Did I miss it? The wrestling business is all-consuming. When I walked away from it, it was like I'd left a part of my soul, as if some important part of me had been amputated. Could I tell Ray that sometimes I walked around the empty bar and cut promos on non-existent opponents? Could I tell him that sometimes I still tried my old wrestling trunks and boots on? Sucked in my gut and pretended that I wasn't fifty-something years old, acting like a kid playing dress-up. Sometimes I looked in the mirror at my own scarred forehead and wondered why I'd done it.

And then I'd think about the crowd screaming for my head. I'd think about the lights and the sweat and the blood. I'd remember the flights and the food and the booze and the women. Every morning when I woke up, I was in pain. My neck, my back, my hips, and my knees ached constantly. And if you asked me if it was worth it, I'd tell you yes, goddamn it, every moment had been worth it.

And Ray wanted to know if I missed it.

"Sometimes," I told him. "Mostly I miss riding around in the Lear jets and limousines."

He laughed.

"I miss that, too. You know what I rented when I got to Atlanta? A goddamned Toyota. We wouldn't have been caught dead in a Toyota."

That made me grin.

"The hell you say. I saw you pull up one night in Meridian, Mississippi, in an AMC Gremlin."

Ray tossed off the rest of his drink.

"That was different. I drove the damned Mercedes off that levee by accident, you know that. Left the keys in it, too. I wonder whatever happened to it?"

That was the life, right there. It was the 1980s and the era of conspicuous consumption. If Ray wrecked a car, he went out and leased another one. He didn't finance anything. He didn't have to. He was making a million dollars a year as the world champion and flying into St. Louis, Portland, San Francisco, Dallas, Tampa, Atlanta. The road was his home, and the money piled up. I'd been in the business for a couple of years myself before we met, and I was bringing home a thousand a week in a little backwater promotion based out of Pensacola, Florida. When Ray pulled up to the arena in that Gremlin, it changed my life.

Ron Baskins was the promoter, a lanky Tennessee hillbilly who'd bought the territory from his cousin and was busy upgrading everything from the rings we used to the arenas we ran. He wanted everything to be first-class, but on a budget. So he paid to have the world champion come into the territory every time he could get dates for him. Ray usually drove himself from town to town, but when he wrecked that Mercedes, Baskins approached me in the locker room and asked if I'd drive the champ for the rest of the tour.

Back in those days, driving the champion around was considered an honor, and I was glad to take on the duty. But with Ray, it was also a bit of a trial. He never slept. After the matches, we'd stop at the nearest gas station and buy a case of beer. By the time we got to Ray's hotel, he'd be lubricated and ready to hit the bars for a couple of hours. But a couple of hours was never enough. We'd find ourselves closing the place down and bringing the party back to Ray's room, where he'd finally fall asleep at six in the morning.

Those drives—and those days—were long. Ray would catch a few hours of sleep in the hotel, work out, and then sleep in the back seat while I drove him to the next stop. There were days that were nothing more than a blur, where I'd had as little sleep as him, but I was the one who was behind the wheel, struggling to keep my eyes open all the time. But I did the job for him, got him to the arenas safe and sound, and kept up with him on the nights when the neon called and nobody went to bed. It also helped that he liked my work in the ring and on the microphone. So when a job opened up in his home territory, he pulled a few strings and I was in.

That's when the craziness really started.

Ray would walk out onto the set of Unlimited Championship Wrestling, dressed in a tailored navy blazer and gray slacks. His tasseled loafers probably cost more than my first car. His crisp white shirt shone on the monitor like an angel's wings. He'd hold the title belt in two hands, proudly displaying the world championship for the fans to see and appreciate. And then he'd talk the fans into the building. He'd get them to give up their hard-earned coin to go watch the world's heavyweight wrestling champion.

And then he'd add a little something extra.

"Now, tomorrow night, I'll be in Las Vegas, Nevada, staying at the Sands Resort and Casino, darlin'. I'll have my best friend, Alex Donovan, with me. And I want all you young ladies to know that if you're between the ages of 18 and 28, we'll be looking for some company. No husbands or boyfriends allowed. Leave 'em at home, girls, and you'll have the time of your lives."

The next night, we showed them why we belonged in Sin City. There were so many women in the hotel lobby that we had to fight to get up to the room. Eight young women made it into the elevator with us, and one of them was sporting a black eye. Ray's shirt was torn, and his belt was missing. The fly on his slacks was open. I'd been groped, kissed, and hugged. One of my shoes was missing.

"Jesus Christ," I said. "I think I had more sex in that lobby than I've ever had in my life."

One of the women on the elevator looked at me with cool brown eyes and said "You ain't seen nothing yet."

Her name was Pam, and she had me naked before we ever got to the room. Lord knows I went willingly enough, and by the time we stepped inside Ray's suite, she'd shed all of her clothes, too …

That was the start, and there were hundreds of nights like it afterward. Ray wasn't just the life of the party, he was the party.

One time I woke up in the same bed with him, the bodies of three women separating us. Neither of us remembered what happened. We never mentioned it.

And I left all of that behind. It'd been five years since I set foot in the ring. I wasn't too injured. Wasn't too old. I was just done. There comes a day when you realize that you look like shit in your trunks, that no amount of good lighting can hide the toll that the road and the bumps and the bruises and that kind of life takes on you. When that happens, you have to get out.

In my saner moments, I was glad I'd gotten out when I did; it was too easy to see myself in Ray Wilder's shoes, riding an endless loop of appearances around the country and the world, spending money faster than I could make it so that the road became a treadmill I could never get off. Ray's nickname was 'Wild Child,' and it fit him. He often told people that he'd never retire from the business. The truth was that he couldn't. He was a wrestler. He didn't know how to do anything else.

We sat at the bar for a couple of hours, old friends passing the time together, but he never told me what was on his mind. Eventually, the bottle of Irish was done, and so was I. Ray stood up from the bar to put on his coat. Other than a slight reddening of his eyes, I couldn't see that the alcohol had much effect on him. I wobbled him to the door, unlocked it, and opened it. He walked outside, but turned around to hug me before he left. "I wanted to talk to you about something," he said. "I don't—"

The gunshot sounded loud, and blood and brain matter sprayed my face. I threw up my arm, but not in time. I should have closed my eyes. I watched my best friend fall across the threshold of the bar I owned, saw half of his head missing. His bleached blonde hair was soaked with blood and his one good pale blue eye rolled in its socket and his Gucci loafers beat an unsteady beat against the floor. His breath hitched, and hitched again. I watched his chest. Somewhere, someone was moaning "No. No. No." over and over again, and it took me a minute to realize that it was me. I grabbed Ray's hand, squeezing, begging him to squeeze my fingers back, to let me know that he knew I was there. And then his chest stopped moving.

Someone must have called 911. I don't know who. I couldn't do it. I kept holding Ray's hand. As long as I held onto him, he wasn't really gone. The paramedics finally pried my hand loose from his and moved me to one of the straight-backed chairs near the stage. They checked me for injuries while I watched them load Ray's body into an ambulance. I don't remember if I responded. When it pulled away, there was no siren. That's when I accepted that my best friend was dead. He'd been murdered right in front of me, and I didn't do anything about it. I watched the crime scene people come and take measurements, pictures, the whole nine yards. Time passed. I'm not sure how much, but the dark night sky was lightening toward purple by the time they were done. I sat in the chair and didn't move. Didn't speak. Didn't do anything. I could have called someone, I suppose, but it didn't seem to matter much now.

"He's in shock," one of the paramedics told a plain-clothed cop. "I don't think you're going to get much out of him."

"I'm fine," I said. My voice sounded very far away, as if it were coming from underwater. The cop asked for my ID, and I dug my wallet out of my back pocket and passed it over. He looked, saw my name, and recognized it from the name on the pub door. I didn't say anything else.

"Sure you are," the cop said. "Have you got keys for this place, Mr. Donovan?"

I did. Somewhere. The paramedic found them in my right front pocket. She took them and passed them over to the cop. The two of them helped me up and then we went outside, and I watched them lock up. They ushered me toward the back of a second ambulance.

"No," I said.

"You need to go to the hospital," the paramedic said. Her name tag said 'Styes' in bold, black, blocky letters.

"No."

"Sir, you're in shock."

"Him," I pointed at the cop. "I'll go with him."

They exchanged glances. "Hell, I gotta question him anyway," the cop said, and escorted me to his car. I got in the back, ducking my head to keep from smacking it against the low window frame. The cop shut the door behind me, and I looked back at my bar. Donovan's Public House in flowing red neon. It should've meant something to me, but the sign felt unfamiliar somehow, as if either it or I had become untethered from reality. I leaned against the back seat of the cop cruiser and closed my eyes. I didn't know where we were going next.

TWO

Aug. 3, 1983
The Houston County Farm Center
Dothan, Alabama

I WAS GLAD to see Ray Wilder on the card, if for no other reason than I knew the bump from his appearance would put my paycheck over two grand for the week. I was wrestling Jorge Calderon for the Alabama heavyweight championship, and we were the semi-main. That meant I had a lot of time to hang out with Ray in the dressing room. That year he was drinking Jack Daniels with a splash of Coca-Cola.

We were talking about my angle with Calderon. We were going around the loop with a gimmick billed as an Indian strap match, and I knew it was going to be physically tough. We'd have to hit each other hard with the leather so that the fans could see the stripes on our bodies. I wasn't going to have a hard time working up some anger at Calderon, either. He'd gotten into Ron Baskins' ear and told him that I should get some juice for him every night around the loop. I hated blading myself—I always thought it was unnecessary. What we were doing was taxing enough on our bodies.

Ray saw it differently. He wanted to know who was going over, meaning who was winning the match. When I told him I was, he grinned and told me there wouldn't be any problem.

"You give him the juice," he said. "Let him open you up early so the sweat mixes with it and the blood looks like it's ten times worse. Let the marks see that you don't like the sight of your own blood. It'll make them happy."

I nodded along. I was still mad at Calderon. Politicking the bookers and promoters was never my strong suit. All I wanted to do was wrestle.

"When you get your heat, you beat the living shit out of him," Ray said. "Don't try to work with the strap, don't hold back. Hit that motherfucker as hard as you can. When you pin him, that's when you whisper in his ear."

"Yeah? What do I tell him?"

"You say 'Same thing tomorrow night, Jorge?'"

So that's what I did. The Farm Center was a great arena, five thousand seats when it was set up for wrestling. And when the world champion was in the house, the place was always packed. The floor was red clay packed hard like an old-fashioned tennis court, the air so dense with humidity and cigarette smoke that just breathing normally made your lungs burn. I went out there under the lights, sweating before I ever wiped my feet on the apron of the ring.

When Jorge hit me square in the forehead, I went down on my stomach and used the little corner of razor blade that I'd taped to my index finger. The cut wasn't big, but I'd had some beer beforehand, and a couple of aspirins, so the juice flowed pretty good. We went around for a few minutes, letting the marks see the crimson mask, and then I started strapping him, much to the dismay of the crowd. Calderon was furious, but he took the whipping like a man. I'd bled for him, and he knew I had to lay the shots with the strap in there, in order to make it look as real as possible. I was grinning all the way back to the dressing room, my body streaked with sweat and a dusting of fine red clay that hung in the air when the building really got going. I shared a handshake with Ray before he went out for his match against local legend Johnnyboy Stevens.

I showered quickly, getting the blood off, and used super glue to close the cut on my forehead. I checked it in the mirror ... it wasn't a big cut, but it was pretty deep. It'd be easy to open up in the next match with Calderon. When I was dressed, I went out to watch Ray and Johnnyboy.

The first thing I noticed was that the ringside fans were all standing. They'd pushed the security railing in toward the ring. The off-duty sheriff's deputies who had been hired as security were trying to keep the crowd back, but not having much success. In the ring, Ray Wilder had Johnnyboy Stevens down on his back and was holding Stevens' feet wide apart. Usually, a wrestler will stomp on his opponent's solar plexus from that position, and then play to the crowd. That way, even if the stomp is harder than intended, the other guy has time to recover. But that's not what the Wild Child did. He hauled back and punted Johnnyboy right in the balls. Didn't pull the kick at all, just a straight-out shot to the nuts. Stevens screamed and clamped his hands between his thighs, his grimace of pain etched so deep that it should have been carved on a mountain somewhere. He tried to crawl away, but Ray wasn't having any of it. He mounted Johnnyboy and was punching him in the head. They were real punches, too. I could see that from the dark corner of the arena where I stood. Something had gone wrong, and the match had turned into a shoot.

Ray used the middle knuckle of his right hand to open a cut on Johnnyboy's forehead, and then quite deliberately, he busted the man's eyebrow, splitting it open to the bone and showering the ringside onlookers in blood and gore.

By this time, Johnnyboy was screaming "My eye! My eye! He's going for my eye!"

The crowd surged forward, and I knew Ray was in trouble. I don't remember moving toward the ring, but I must've, because the next thing I knew, I'd taken a folding chair out of some mark's hands and was swinging it around my head and swinging it around my head like a berserker wielding a battle axe, clearing a path to the ring. The fans parted like the Red Sea before Moses, and I slid under the bottom rope, along with the chair.

Johnnyboy Stevens slithered out the other side of the ring, just happy to get away from the Wild Child. Ray and I stood back-to-back in the middle of the ring until the PA announcer told everyone that Ray had lost due to a disqualification, and the sheriff's deputies finally got things under control. I kept the chair in my hands as we left the ring and remembered to walk slowly toward the locker room. Back in those days, you didn't run from the fans. If you did, they'd chase you, and that could be very bad news.

Once we got back to safety, I could let go of the chair. Except my fingers seemed to be locked around it. My grip was permanent, to the point that I wondered if I'd accidentally super-glued my fingers together while I was repairing the cut on my forehead. I started laughing. So did Ray. None of the other heels—those useless assholes—understood why we were laughing. We had the rancid stink of fear on us. We knew how close things had come to being a truly bad scene. Eventually I released the chair and let it clatter to the floor. Ray went over to his bottle of Jack Daniels and cracked the seal. He took a long pull at the brown liquor, then handed it to me.

I wiped the neck of the bottle with my hand and drank deep. The whiskey burned going down, then blossomed in my stomach. We kept laughing. I started to hand him the bottle, but he waved me off.

"Don't worry about it," he said. "I've got another one in my bag."

We went around through the towns that week: Dothan and Birmingham, Montgomery and Huntsville, Biloxi and Meridian. Johnnyboy Stevens was out of the promotion. He'd tried to double-cross Ray in the ring, tying him up in an amateur move and legitimately trying to pin him for the belt. Ray was larger than

Stevens, and a great deal stronger. He was able to break the hold, reverse it, and begin kicking the shit out of the hometown hero. Instead, Jorge Calderon got moved into the main event with Ray—because no matter how big a pain in the ass Jorge was, he was a great worker, and Ray didn't give a shit about bleeding—and I worked with Brad Thompson, a young up-and-comer who happened to be the son of the territory's booker.

It worked out for everyone. Two months later, Ray called and booked me into Charlotte, North Carolina, and I kissed the Pensacola territory goodbye.

THREE

THE COP'S NAME was Aldeman, and he looked around my age. His uniform was starched and clean, and his infantry-style boots were shined. He had the florid face of a heavy drinker, with a nose like a potato and cheeks that showed every burst capillary from a lifetime on the sauce. I knew the signs. He took my statement, typing it out on what looked to be a 1995-era Gateway computer. The CRT screen flickered uncertainly every few moments. I told him what I could remember, my voice still curiously flat and monotone. The lights in the detective bureau weren't helping, either. The fluorescents made everything look too bright, and the quiet sounds of cops coming and going around me made quiet echoes in my head. Even though I'd only had a little whiskey—at least compared to what Ray and I used to drink—I felt drunk, like I'd start listing to the side if he asked me to stand up.

I asked to go to the bathroom and staggered down the hall to where he pointed. I used the toilet, flushed, and spent a long time running cold water over my face and hands. It was nearly nine a.m. I'd had too much coffee and not enough sleep, and my fingers trembled when I held them in front of my face. I shut off

17

the faucet and dried my hands on a paper towel. When I got back to Aldeman's desk, he told me I could go home if I wanted. I just looked at him.

"I mean it," he said. "There's nothing else for you to do here."

I shoved my hands into my pockets, tilted my head to the side a little. All I wanted to do was go home and get some sleep, but it felt like there had to be more.

"Don't you need me to identify the body? I had seen a lot of cop shows. I knew how it went.

Aldeman shook his head.

"We've got your statement. We got your security tape. We know who the victim is. I've got a couple guys working on notifying next of kin right now, but that seems to be going slow. Anything you can think of to help there?"

I told him no. Ray didn't have family, really, just a succession of ex-wives to whom he owed varying amounts of alimony. His kids didn't know him. One or two of them might be sad he was dead. Some of them would be glad. They'd all be disappointed the gravy train had stopped. Aldeman told me that he was sorry for my loss, and then he got a uniformed cop to drive me back to Five Points.

"Case like this," he said before handing me off to the other cop, "is a high-profile crime. Something will break. We'll get whoever did this."

I didn't share his confidence. Throughout most of my career, almost everyone had considered me Ray's enforcer, the guy who would lay his body on the line to protect Ray. When it had mattered most, I had frozen. I couldn't remember a goddamn thing except Ray lying there in my arms, half his head blown off, the fine mist of blood and brain matter coating my face and neck.

Ray was dead, and I hadn't done anything. Even more: I could have been dead, too. I'd frozen out there on the street. Ten years ago—hell, five years ago—that wouldn't have happened. Somewhere along there, I had gotten old.

When the uniformed cop touched my shoulder, I woke with

a start. The ten-minute drive back to the pub had been too far, and I'd fallen asleep with my forehead pressed against the cool window. I thanked the kid and got out of the cruiser. There was no way I could bring myself to unlock the front door of the pub, step over the blood and the chalk outline of my friend, so I went up the back entrance, rattling up a long metal flight of stairs to the door of my apartment.

Inside, it was dark. I didn't need lights, though. The apartment was large, about half of the third floor of the building, with floor-to-ceiling windows that let in a lot of light. The combination dining and living area was populated with a lot of low, comfortable furniture, the floors textured with Asian-style rugs. A kitchen I rarely used was an afterthought, like a puppy no one wanted. The walls were off-white, and the only real decorations were a couple of posters in metal frames. One showed Ray and me with the world tag team titles. The other showed me with the world TV title around my waist. Two bedrooms opened off of opposite sides of the living area. I stumbled to the kitchen and started to put on some coffee, but thought better of it. I was already overcaffeinated and jittery.

Instead, I went to the bedroom. On the wall, in a shadow box, the world TV title belt glittered. When the promoters decided to do away with the championship, Ray copped it for me. It was the highest I'd ever gone as a singles wrestler, and the gesture—that he'd thought enough of me to make it—meant a lot to me. I stood there looking at the belt for a while, an uneasy buzz in my head and stomach.

The light on my answering machine blinked steadily like a metronome, showing thirty-six missed calls and a dozen messages. I'm old-school enough that I keep a landline. That's the number I give out to everyone. I sat down on the bed to listen to the messages, but the weight of everything threatened to press me down and smother me with sleep. I stripped down and showered, and that worked to bring me back to life a little. I stayed under the spray for a long time, letting the stink of fear and blood and rancid coffee rinse away. The hot water ran out, but I didn't let the cold drive me away. Little frozen needles burned against my skin. When I'd had enough, I shut everything off and toweled dry.

The message light was still blinking when I came out of the shower. I thought about just pulling the plug on the whole thing, letting it all die with an annoying flicker. The messages would still be there when I wanted to hear them. But there's something in me that feels obsessive-compulsive. I can't let messages go unheard or texts stay on read. I pushed the button and listened to every reporter in the metro area give me their condolences and then ask for an interview. I shook my head. I knew they were only doing their jobs, but it felt predatory to me.

Even if it hadn't felt that way, I wouldn't have called a reporter back. I spent all of my adult life in a business that shuns honesty, that turns away from light shined on it like a cockroach scrambling for a corner when the lights come on. Talking to the press wasn't even a possibility in my world. Wrestling's kayfabe—the idea that you don't tell anyone anything about the inside workings of the business—was our version of the Mafia's omertà.

Sure, the wrestling business has changed. Everyone knows it's "fake" now. But say it's fake to the boys with busted-up backs, with brains that are scrambled from too many chair shots to the dome. Say it to the guys who went bankrupt because they had to have hips or shoulders replaced because of all the damage they took and no insurance company in the goddamn world will touch them. Say it's fake to the guys who died from too much booze or too many pills. Tell it to the boys who ran off the goddamn road at three in the morning just trying to make it back home from a show in some shitty town no one else but one of us 'rasslers had ever heard of, just because we were booked there.

Every month—sometimes every week—I get guys coming into the pub who want to prove they're tough, or who want to mouth off to the ex-wrestler about how wrestling is fake. They usually go out the door feet-first and semiconscious.

I rubbed scratchy palms over weary eyes. No idea what to do next. I had to do something to clear my head. I deleted all of the messages until I came to the last one. A voice I hadn't heard in more than a decade spoke to me in the dark bedroom, and despite myself, gooseflesh rose on my bare arms and legs.

"Donovan, it's Malone Tomlinson," he said, as if I wouldn't have recognized his voice in my sleep. "I'm sorry as hell to hear about Ray, pal. We're gonna do something for him on TV, put up a tribute on the Web. Come down to Boutwell this afternoon. I know you know where it is."

Even in my groggy state, I noted that Malone hadn't asked me to come. He'd told me to. Malone was like that.

Malone Tomlinson ran Unlimited Championship Wrestling. He was a billionaire a couple of times over, taking the regional company that his father had sold him and taking it national, blowing up a decades-long arrangement between promoters. Wrestling had been broken into fiefdoms, with each promoter a small king in a crumbling castle. Other promoters didn't run against the hometown promoters. It simply wasn't done. For years, a delicate balance between promoters held. But Malone didn't care about the back-room handshake deals that kept most of the wrestling business running. When he went national, he threw a grenade into the back room and blew it all up. He drove competitors out of business with a ruthlessness that bordered on sociopathy. He was shameless. When Bill Cunningham committed suicide because of Tomlinson's predatory tactics, Malone sent a wreath of flowers to the funeral with a ribbon that read "Better luck next time."

The last time I'd talked with Malone had been just before I opened Donovan's Public House. He'd looked at me with his direct, unsettling gaze, and told me that I might be done with the wrestling business, but he didn't believe it was done with me.

It looked like he was right. UCW was at the Boutwell, and I

would show up. No one in Birmingham held a grudge against Ray—no one that I knew about, anyway—so that meant that his killer was somehow connected to Malone Tomlinson's wrestling promotion. Ray needed someone to care about him, to find out who had killed him. I'd had his back countless times over the years, and he'd had mine, too. Now it looked like I'd get one last chance to stand up for him.

I shaved carefully. I'm not sure I could have taken it if I'd cut myself. And then I went to bed. I was sure I wouldn't be able to sleep, that it would be as elusive as a ghost. But the darkness came up and choked me out before my head ever hit the pillow.

FOUR

June 17, 1984
Wheeling, West Virginia

DEAN "THE KILLER" Miller was a promoter's wet dream: Six feet, three inches, narrow hips and wide shoulders, wavy blond hair and a thick mustache that curled down at the corners of his mouth and made him look more intense than he already was. He was good-looking enough for the women to swoon over, and manly enough that the guys didn't feel too weird about cheering for him.

We were backstage, and someone had a deck of cards. Someone always had a deck in those days. We played hearts or spades in the locker room, or even cribbage if someone had a board. Never poker. Bill Cunningham, the promoter for National Championship Wrestling, had a standing rule about that: You want to start a fight, go do it on your own time.

So no poker in the locker room.

That never mattered to Ray, though.

"I usually poke her somewhere else, if you know what the Wild Child means."

He was loud and abrasive and funny as hell. And he was the world champion. People came to see him, and to see him get beat. That didn't happen often, but the fans had gotten behind Killer

23

Miller, who was in his first year in the business and already getting a run at the top of the card. He was money, and the office knew it. Tonight Miller and Ray would work the main event, while I was responsible for dragging a second-generation French Canadian kid to a halfway passable match right after intermission.

We were playing spades at a rickety folding table with Jackie and Tommy, the Fulltones. They were part-time wrestlers and part-time soul singers, real brothers who had grown up in Memphis on a diet of slow-cooked ribs and sweet Delta blues in equal measure. They'd managed to win the promotion's tag team titles, and they were the first Black guys to do so. They busted their ass in the ring, and then they drank all night. Ray must've thought they were long-lost family members.

The Killer came over, interrupting our game to shake hands, nearly crushing my knuckles to dust. I didn't sell it, though. When he turned and stuck his hand out to Ray, I grinned. If you didn't know the Wild Child well, you couldn't tell anything was wrong. But he was giving me a big-eyed stare over Miller's shoulder while the kid mumbled the same thing that every rookie ever said to Ray Wilder.

"Thank you, sir —"

"It's an honor —"

"I appreciate the opportunity —"

When Miller finally went on his way, Jackie grinned at me. Ray looked troubled. He always lived up to his nickname, but the Wild Child also had a damned good head for the business. One of the Fulltones, I forget which one, shuffled, his dark brown hands flickering over the cards in the uncertain and ugly yellow light of the locker room. He offered Ray the cut, but the champ wasn't interested. The Fulltones dealt like he sang: smooth and sure. A nearly forgotten Newport cigarette hung in the corner of his mouth.

"Fingers still work?"

"Barely," I said. "Kid's got Vise-Grips for hands."

"Ain't nothin' broke, though?" He took a hard drag on his cigarette, held the smoke for a long moment, and blew a cloud of white-gray fumes, adding it to the layer of smog that hung in the locker room.

I shook my head.

"See, he likes you. We gonna play them cards or fuck around some more, champ?"

We picked up our cards. Tommy bid two, and Jackie bid three. I was trying to figure out what the hell I was gonna do with no aces or kings when Ray threw his cards down and told Jackie to get someone to sit in for us.

"Come on," he said. "We gotta go see Cunningham."

Bill Cunningham didn't make every town; he had road agents for that, the guys who rode from town to town as if they were one of the boys. Often, they were ex-wrestlers themselves. They were responsible for pretty much everything, from the gate receipts to making sure the building stayed in one piece if the locker room got rowdy. But Wheeling was a good town. The crowds were rowdy and we were drawing nearly a hundred grand a show, so Cunningham was keeping a close eye on the place.

His office was just a small room off of the back hallway with easy access to an exit door. Cunningham could step out of his office, cross the hall, and hit the door anytime he wanted to. He had a Lincoln Continental parked outside and a driver ready to take him back to Charlotte whenever Bill said go.

Ray was in his ring gear: Red trunks with matching knee pads and wrestling boots that had RW monogrammed on them in flowing white script. He wore a Gold's Gym T-shirt, and his hair was tied back with a sequined bandanna. I trailed along with him, my hands tucked into the pockets of my windbreaker. I held a roll of quarters in my left fist in case of trouble.

Ray didn't bother knocking. He never did. He was the world champion, and even though he was humble in the locker room, he also knew that carrying the belt gave him a lot of stroke.

Cunningham looked up from whatever he was doing, ready to be irritated. When he realized it was Ray, his face smoothed into a grin.

"What's going on, champ? Sit down."

Ray didn't sit. He'd worked himself up on the way down the hall. I knew what he was doing by then: he was cutting a promo to himself, gearing up for whatever imaginary fight he was about to have with the promoter.

"Have I ever refused to do business?"

Cunningham looked shocked.

"What?" He asked, turning to me. I stayed stone-faced. This—whatever this was—was between them. "What are you talking about? Of course you do business."

"That's right," Ray said. "I want you to remember this. I came here in 1978, and I never said no. I done everything you asked, I never once said no when the office asked me to do the favor—"

Cunningham stood up, too, and I could feel the tension in the room ratchet up a couple of notches.

"You mean when I asked you to do the favor."

Ray shrugged.

"That's right, but I never said no, did I? I ever even politick a little?"

Cunningham paused before he answered, and the quiet hung heavy and ripe in the room.

"Well, yeah," he said finally, "you have—but not too much."

Ray started to grin, then, and I relaxed a little.

"Your new boy—Killer Miller? He's a fuckin' menace. Green as a goddamn pepper tree. Are you trying to get me killed? Is that it?"

"The fans like him."

"The fans like what you tell them to like."

"You don't want to work him? Is that it? We advertised the main event, Ray. We can't refund tickets just because you're scared of the kid."

Ray drew back as if he'd been slapped. A hard spot of color

shone on each of his cheeks, but the rest of his face was as white as I'd ever seen it.

"I'm not going to dignify that," he said. He took a deep breath. "My concern is not tonight. My concern is that he doesn't know what he's doing, and one of us will get hurt."

He looked directly at Cunningham then. "And if one of us gets hurt, I guarantee it's not going to be me."

Bill Cunningham sat down and rubbed his face with both hands. There was a coffee pot on a side table, and he poured himself a cup without offering any to Ray or me. He was silent while he stirred in sugar and creamer. Then he looked at us.

"You think he could cross us?"

"I think he's a kid who doesn't know what he's doing. He needs someone to smarten him up, and it doesn't need to be me."

Cunningham finally nodded, more to himself than to either of us.

"All right," he said. "I still want the match. But take your gorilla here"—he motioned toward me—"and have him at ringside. Any funny stuff, you end it. Quick."

When we went out that night, I accompanied Ray, walking just outside the spotlight where he stood alone. That was how things were with Ray Wilder. He shone so brightly that no matter how good you were, you were in the shadows compared to him. I wore a satin warm-up jacket that said Ribera Steakhouse on the back, with a stylized logo of a bull on the front. In my pocket I had a small length of pig iron just big enough for my fist. Better than a roll of quarters.

When the match started, I could tell that something was off. Other than his flamboyant hair and his signature strut, the Wild Child was known in the locker room as a great seller. 'Selling' the offense of your opponent is one of the key components of being a great wrestler. Everyone said that Ray could make a broomstick look good, but that night Ray had it in mind to show Bill

Cunningham and Killer Miller what it could be like when the champ was pissed.

The Wild Child was known for his hour-long matches. He prided himself on going into the ring with anyone from any territory and making them look like a million dollars. That night, Ray made Miller look silly at every opportunity. When his opponent lifted him for a body slam, Ray wriggled out and slid over Miller's shoulder. Miller turned around, confused, and Ray threw him for real with a headlock takeover.

The referee, sensing that something was wrong, dropped down to count Miller's shoulders. The kid was built like a horse, though. He was young and strong, and his gym-pretty muscles gleamed under the house lights.

Ray didn't cooperate with anything that Miller tried, and the kid was so green that he didn't know what to do. He was strong and he was in shape, maybe five years younger than me. There was a point where he could have maybe turned the tables on Ray, just from sheer size and power. But Ray wasn't really shooting on the kid. He was fucking with him, making him look bad.

And the fans noticed. Ray was a professional in the sense that he would never expose the business, but he was exposing Miller. The fans expected the Killer to win, or at least to bounce the Wild Child from pillar to post. Instead, Miller was out of breath and trembling from nervousness and anger. He hadn't been in the wrestling business long, but he knew what Ray was doing. He just didn't know how to stop it. Ray took him down and kept him on the mat, shooting a half nelson and coupling that with a hammerlock. The champ basically rolled Miller around the ring like a donut. I put my head down on the apron of the ring and covered my face in my hands so that no one could see me laughing. When the fans started cheering Ray instead of Miller, the kid looked at the crowd, his face hurt and confused.

After twelve minutes, I'd seen enough. I climbed into the ring and punched the kid in the jaw as hard as I could, right in front of the referee. I had the pig iron clamped tight in my fist, making it hard and heavy as a brick. I swung, and the kid looked almost grateful to see the shot coming. Killer Miller went down and out, Ray was disqualified, and we hightailed it back to the locker room with the world title belt held aloft so everyone in the building could see it. The last I saw of Killer Miller, he was flat on his back, unconscious in the middle of the ring. If he ever wrestled another match for Bill Cunningham, I never heard about it.

FIVE

BUSINESS CAME FIRST. Ray was the guy who taught me that while I was coming up in the territory system. Take care of the business aspect of things first, and let the personal stuff wait. This time, taking care of business meant a phone call to my part-time bartender, Casey. I told him I'd be away from the bar, possibly for a few days, and asked him to cover, make sure to get a professional cleaner—someone who had some experience with removing potentially hazardous waste—to wash the front part of the building. Casey would get some extra hours and tips, but he'd also have to be on-site for the beer distributors and their delivery trucks.

Once that was taken care of, I drove two blocks east on Highland Avenue, and then hooked a left onto Richard Arrington Boulevard. Even with traffic picking up, the drive took less than fifteen minutes. I hung a left at the Jefferson County Courthouse, and a right onto 19th Street. Boutwell Auditorium was on the right, a boxy gray building with an unimpressive exterior. But it seated nearly six thousand people, and for more than half a century, wrestling had been coming to the Boutwell on Monday nights. You could see every regional star there, usually presented by Nick Gulas. I hadn't been inside in a long time, but every time I drove past, I smiled at the history of the place. I went around the building and parked underneath the I-20/59 overpass. Wrestlers had been parking there as long as I could remember.

It was like a visit to the old neighborhood. I put my Mustang in a space between a late-model Honda Accord and a Nissan Maxima and beeped the key fob to make sure the doors locked. It was a short walk across an alley to the rear entrance, and you used to have to dodge the autograph seekers and the photographers and the guys who just wanted to see if those 'rasslers were as tough as they looked on TV. But those were the old days. Now they had security everywhere. You'd think it would be hard to get backstage, and normally you'd be right. But I'm not just another pretty face.

It also helped that I spotted Scotty Prichard behind the building, taking a quick smoke break. He saw me, held the smoke from the jay in his lungs as long as he could, and then breathed out the sweet, fragrant smoke in a gigantic huff.

"Can't you get in trouble for that?" I asked, but Scotty shook his head. He reached for my hand, and we shook.

"Not anymore. They had too many guys in the main event busted for weed, so they had to lighten up."

He offered me a hit, but I declined. I didn't want my mind any more altered than it already was. He took in another big drag, the flaming tip of the little cigarette glowing deep red. He held the smoke a little longer this time, and breathed out a little easier. I waited. I didn't want to wave the fumes away, but I really wanted to get inside the building.

"I heard about Ray," he said at last. "Terrible."

"Yeah," I said. What else was there to say?

Scotty took one last drag, then flipped what was left of the joint away into the grass near the corner of the building, where it smoldered for a moment, then went out.

"Malone ask you to come?"

"Yeah."

"Come on," he said. "I know the boys will want to see you."

The boys. It was what wrestlers always called themselves to distinguish themselves from the guys who worked in the promoter's office. Working stiffs in the locker room, nobody better than anybody else. That was us. Even guys like Ray, who had the reputation outside the ring, were respectful to one another in the locker room. If you weren't, it was a good way to make enemies.

I didn't really want to see anyone. I was far enough out of the business that most of the kids on the roster wouldn't know who I was anyway. And then there was the memory of Ray, his last moments, weighing heavy in my chest. I wanted to go back to the bar and get roaring drunk, tell Ray Wilder stories, and pick a fight with anybody who even looked at me wrong. Instead, Scott Prichard was guiding me from the loading dock to the backstage area, as if in the last few years I'd forgotten where everything was. He found a stooge—I think they call them production assistants now—and got me a laminated backstage pass. I felt like a horse's ass wearing it, but I kept it on anyway.

To my left were a couple of large dressing rooms, complete with makeup counters and long mirrors lit by lines of high-watt bulbs. Scott trailed along behind me as I walked in. There were metal folding chairs scattered around, and a lot of the younger guys were busy playing hand-held video games, or texting on their phones, building their "brand" on social media. Everyone seemed isolated in their own little bubble.

It felt much different than five or ten years before. We'd been more social, I think. We played cards together, and dominoes if someone really felt like throwing down in the locker room. Of course, that had been before social media had been a thing. No tweets to send, no Toks to Tik, no streams with thousands of fans tuning in to watch us play video games.

I never wanted to sound like one of those old guys who hangs around too long. The kids in the locker room were probably a lot healthier than we were. They were undoubtedly better athletes. To a person, they looked carved from stone, chiseled by a thoughtful and benevolent creator. Not a beer belly in sight. I bet nobody was sneaking nips from a bottle of whiskey or a little bump of cocaine to get them up for a promo or match, either. I wondered how many of them carried guns in their bags like we used to and then decided the number had to be zero or close to it.

When I broke into the territories, we used to spend hours upon hours in a car, town to town. The new breed spent maybe even longer traveling, but a lot of it was by plane. Having to go through multiple security checkpoints in any given week probably put a damper on carrying anything to defend yourself.

Scott introduced me around, and I spent a few minutes shaking hands and making nice. A funny thing about the wrestling business: In many ways, it is as steeped in its traditions as baseball. And as conservative. When you get to the arena, you shake hands with every one of the boys you see. The handshake is a sign of respect, and a signal that, yeah, I made it to the next town. I'm still here, boys.

The tradition has changed a little over the years. The old-timers used to give a limp, barely-there handshake, sometimes using only a couple of fingers. It was a signal of how you worked in the ring: that you were going to treat the other wrestler's body with respect. Anyone who tried to crush your grip was looked at with disdain. Not knowing the "secret" handshake meant that you weren't smart to the business.

Scotty led me through Gorilla, the staging area next to the entrance into the arena. Agents and producers were prepping monitors and talking about camera angles for the night's live broadcast. Cables and power cords littered the floor, and silver-hinged road cases had been pushed against every available wall. A weekly live television show is not lightly undertaken. I saw a couple of familiar faces here and there, but they were busy, so I just nodded as we passed. One of the techs was Sam Smith, whose job was to cue theme music for each wrestler's entrance. He grinned at me and nudged another tech. I couldn't catch what he said, but when Scotty and I paused at the curtain, my old music began to play over the house speakers.

"Son of a bitch," I said. I couldn't help but laugh.

Scotty slapped me on the back and said "Go." I stepped through the curtain and onto the stage for the first time in what felt like forever.

Ghosts of crowds past seemed to cheer for a long and silent moment, and spotlights that shined only in my memory transfixed me there on the stage.

The Boutwell can hold almost six thousand people when it's set up for wrestling, and for just a moment when I stepped out to my music, it felt like the place was once again full, every seat in the place filled by someone who wanted my blood. But when I looked—really looked—there was no one there. The ghosts were all in my memory. It was still hours before the doors would open to the public, and metal folding chairs sat mute and empty in lines so straight they looked like soldiers at attention, awaiting orders.

Around the ring, it was different. There were twenty or so of the boys—and some girls—hanging out there. Some of them were talking to agents and camera operators, laying out matches, timing sequences, generally getting ready for the show. It was a much more complicated affair than when I'd been an active wrestler. Back then, everything had to look real, so you never had a chance to go over your match in the ring prior to the show. If some janitor or security guard saw you being chummy with your opponent before the show, it could be a firing offense.

And now everyone in the ring was looking at me.

If you're a wrestler—even a broken-down has-been like me—you never just walk to the ring. The entranceway is a long, shallow ramp to the floor of the arena, so you gather momentum as you go. By the time I hit the lower level, I was almost jogging.

Jesus, it had been a long time. I went up the steps as though my knees didn't bother me and stepped through the ropes like I still belonged in the ring.

I heard someone scream my name about the same time a five-foot tornado with pink hair and a face full of stage makeup hit me and wrapped her arms around my waist. Penny Baker lifted me off the mat, no easy feat, and crushed my ribs with a hug.

"What the hell are you doing here?" She asked, pushing herself away to hold me at arms length and look me up and down. I did the same. Penny had been an Olympic weightlifting hopeful at one point, and she was nothing but muscle. Her blonde hair ended in pink pigtails, and her face looked young and fresh without the heavy shadow and false eyelashes a professional makeup artist would apply later. I grinned down at her—I couldn't help it, because Penny was such a spark—and then remembered why I was there.

"Put me down, kid," I said. "People will talk."

"They'll say I kicked your ass again. You wanna go grab some food with Kat and me?"

Penny Baker and Katherine Ash had been a couple as long as I'd known them. Kat was Katarina the Great when she was in the ring. Where Penny was short and stout, Kat's was tall and lithe. Every woman in the wrestling business wore a spray-on tan except for Kat, whose milky-white skin contrasted with her black hair and dark eyes. To see Katherine Ash in passing was to give yourself whiplash. You couldn't help but look again. Kat and Ray had been good friends … and for about two weeks while Penny and Kat were having some trouble, they had been more than friendly.

"Maybe later," I said. "I'm here about Ray."

"Oh, God. Malone told us. It happened at your place, didn't it?"

"Yeah. Someone laid for him."

"Awful," Penny said, but she was already reaching for a mirror to check her makeup for smudges. "I'm so sorry, Alex."

"She's the only one," someone said, and I turned. Marcus Digger—of course they called him Gravedigger—stood in the middle of the ring. He was wearing sweats and a tank top pulled tight over a massive chest. His shoulders shined under the house lights as if they'd been oiled. And they probably had. Wrestling is a cosmetic business.

"What did you say?"

"You heard me," Digger said, moving closer to me. "Ray thought he was a legend, that he could get away with anything. Well, fuck him. We don't need any more old-timers out here telling us what we're doing wrong. You show me where the body is so I can go piss on it."

Marcus Digger stood seven inches taller than my five-eleven, and he probably had forty pounds on me. I was always blocky, even when I was wrestling a full-time schedule, but next to Digger, I felt small and out of shape. Retirement had helped some pounds pile on. But I'd never backed down from an asshole with pretty-boy gym muscles, and I wasn't planning to now, either.

I squared up to Digger and folded my hands together in front of my belt buckle, pressing hard against my own grip with my bottom hand. I kept the pressure there, but didn't let the strain show on my face.

"Ray Wilder was my friend," I said, keeping my voice as calm as I could. Beside me, Penny Baker moved out of the way. She could tell something was coming. "On your best day, you couldn't lace his boots."

Digger stepped closer, and when he did, I opened my left hand, releasing the pressure on my right fist and letting it fly forward, almost of its own volition. It hit Digger right under the nose. Blood spurted, and one of his front teeth fell onto the canvas, root and all. He staggered back, his hands cupping his mouth and nose. Tears streamed down his cheeks. While his hands were up, I kicked him in the groin. I didn't feel bad about it. He was probably twenty years younger than me, and I didn't want to have to roll around on the mat with him. Digger screamed in pain and crumpled to his hands and knees, his mouth drawn down in a rictus of pain. I stepped on his ankle while he was down, and he cried out again.

It wasn't enough. I started forward, set on stomping Marcus Digger to death, when rough hands grabbed me and pulled me back. I struggled for a moment, letting the red rage of my thoughts take me, but by that time security had moved into the ring and pushed me to a corner where they could hold me against the turnbuckle.

Once security had me cornered, I relaxed. No need to fight after that, put up some kind of show. Someone had found a cup of milk at catering, and they dropped Digger's tooth into it to try to save it. Digger was trying to rise, but that's a difficult thing to do when your testicles are somewhere north of your navel. He was on his feet now, favoring the leg I'd stepped on. I tensed in case he decided to come for me. It was what I would have done if someone had just embarrassed me in front of the boys. I wasn't one of the wrestlers now; the locker room wasn't mine anymore. Instead I was an outsider, an interloper who no longer belonged in the fraternity.

SIX

April 3, 1987
Municipal Auditorium
Houma, Louisiana

PEEKY CARMICHAEL SAW them before I did. Peeky was the best referee in the business when it came to rowdy crowds, and Houma was a place where you took your life in your hands just walking to the ring. It didn't matter how many cops were on hand—some shit was always gonna go down in Houma.

Ray and I had won the world tag team titles from the Fulltones the last time we'd been in Houma—and of course we'd cheated to do it— and those Cajuns lost their shit. I was driving Ray everywhere, because that's what I did. The fans down there were so angry that I couldn't just drive to the auditorium. Instead, I had to park at the police station. The cops put us in unmarked cruisers and drove us to the building. They drove up over the curb to drop us off at the door, one long step from car to building, so we didn't even have to see the fans waiting outside.

That night, I had my hands around Jackie Fulltone's throat, and it looked like I was choking the life out of him. His eyes were bugging out in his head, he was gasping, and his arms were flailing bonelessly against the mat.

If I didn't know better, I'd have thought I was killing him, too.

Ray and I were defending the world tag titles against the Fulltones, and they were more than popular in Louisiana and Mississippi. Ray was on the apron, but his attention was split. There was a blonde on the front row directly across from him, and every now and then she'd lift her shirt to show us the goods, and they were very good indeed. Tommy Fulltone didn't know what was going on, so he was holding onto the tag rope in his corner and stomping on the apron of the ring to beseech his brother to rise and make the tag.

The first guy made it into the ring before Peeky could stop him, but the skinny ref put his head down and drove with his legs. His hands locked around the man's ankle and allowed his momentum to drive the shoulder into the side of his leg for a nearly textbook example of an ankle pick. Ray hopped into the ring and drove one booted foot into the interloper's ribs. The air went out of him in a great whoosh. The next kick went into the man's temple, and if the cops hadn't dragged the fool out of the ring, Ray might've killed him.

None of us saw the second guy until Jackie Fulltone whispered "Look out." His eyes widened and a dark shadow rose over my left shoulder, briefly obscuring the arena lights.

There's an art to hitting someone with a steel folding chair and making it look good. You use the flat part of the chair, at the last minute loosening your grip to lessen the impact. It still hurts, but it's not the worst thing in the world, either. And most of the time you're swinging that chair from somewhere that your opponent can see it coming. They can get their hands up to soften the blow even more.

What we don't do: turn the chair sideways and swing the narrow, reinforced edge of it as hard as we can into the back of our opponent's head. But that's what the second fan into the ring did. The chair hit me square on my growing bald spot. The soft skin split and showered me and Jackie Fulltone with blood. I didn't lose consciousness, but I did stagger away from Jackie, dropping to a knee. Ray was still looking out at the asshole that he'd disabled, working the crowd into a frenzy. Peeky waved toward the timekeeper and threw the match out. The bell rang while the announcer proclaimed that there was no decision in our match.

I tried to cover up while a burly farmer in stained overalls and heavy work boots stalked me with the chair held high in his hands. Blood and sweat mixed and ran in a river down my back. Thinking quickly, Jackie yanked the chair out of the fan's hand and came after me. He hit me with the chair and I bailed. Jackie and his brother stood with the fan in the middle of the ring while Ray and I took the world tag belts and fled backstage. Cops boiled into the ring and wrestled the fan to the canvas.

"God DAMN what happened out there?" Ray asked. I didn't have an answer for him. My head was buzzing and everything looked weird and slightly out of focus. About that time, the cops dragged the fan backstage and brought him over to us. His eyes were rolling around in his head and he struggled against the restraints where the cops had cuffed his hands behind his back.

"Listen, man, I'm —"

Sorry, he was going to say. Sorry. Right. He was sorry now that the cops had ahold of him, now that he was standing face-to-face with me. This redneck dirt farmer wasn't wearing anything besides his overalls, and reddish-blonde hair covered most of his shoulders and chest. He was wearing thick wire-frame glasses, and black dirt grimed the creases of his neck.

I hit him in the mouth. His rubbery lips split and the rotted teeth in his mouth broke free of his gums like tumbled-down tombstones. He collapsed, so big and fat that the cops holding him couldn't manage to keep him upright when his knees gave out. The man slithered to the floor, his forehead hitting hard concrete with a sound like an axe handle thumping a watermelon. I kicked him in the face and would have done it again if Ray hadn't stopped me.

"Come on," he said. "Let's go get you fixed up."

The fat man's glasses had fallen to the floor, too, but they were still intact. I stepped on them as I walked away. The crunch when they splintered and broke was satisfying in a way that was nearly orgasmic.

It took seventeen stitches and six staples to close the wound to the back of my head.

SEVEN

MALONE TOMLINSON SAT behind the makeshift desk in his makeshift office. His legs were propped on one corner of the desk, and his feet jiggled his handmade Italian leather shoes. Malone never wore socks; I think it had something to do with growing up in a trailer park in the hills of North Carolina. Technically, he was Malone Tomlinson, Jr., but no one ever called him Junior. His Daddy had run one of the most lucrative wrestling territories in the world, but he let Malone grow up poor, with a single mother. Malone Senior only acknowledged his son once the kid was in his teens.

Maybe that was a kindness. I don't know. The professional wrestling business is hard on relationships, whether it's with your significant other or your children. It's one of the reasons I never married. Nearly every wrestler I know has been married at least twice, with kids they've barely met. I guess sometimes you can repair those bridges, but it seems like an awful lot of work to me.

Regardless, the younger Malone Tomlinson never seemed to get over being ostracized from his father. He went away for short stints at reform school a couple of times as a teen—and then he got shipped off to college at The Citadel, a wannabe West Point for Southerners who had never gotten over the Civil War.

He could've gone into the military. I'm convinced that Malone would've made a great general. His war against the territory promoters was as much a scorched-earth campaign as Sherman's march through Georgia. His temper and his audacity was legendary. Tomlinson had built an empire from his father's own limited holdings. Now, at seventy-something years old, he was an apex predator with nothing left to fight. All of the battles were over, and he was the king of professional wrestling.

And here I was, sitting across a desk from him again, waiting to be scolded like a kid who'd gotten in trouble at school.

"You didn't have to hit him," Malone said. "My biggest star's supposed to cut a promo tonight, how's that gonna go? Dammit, pal, he looks like he could floss with rope."

"I don't know. Maybe it'll make him look tougher. Remember Mad Dog Vachon?"

Maurice "Mad Dog" Vachon had been an Olympic-caliber wrestler before he became a pro. He was always one of the toughest cats around, but once he lost several front teeth and shaved his head, he became an international superstar and a world champion. I'd met Mad Dog a few times toward the end of his career. One time we were on a small plane, a Piper Cub, going from Minneapolis to Omaha, Nebraska. I don't know what Mad Dog had taken before the flight, but he became convinced we were still sitting in the hotel lobby. Afraid he was going to miss the flight, Mad Dog kept trying to get up and get to the door of the plane. Four of us had to hold him down to keep Mad Dog from jumping to his death.

Malone considered my idea, and then dismissed it with a shake of his head.

"It makes him look like a refugee from a homeless shelter," he said. "We'll have to get it fixed."

The room Malone was using for an office was a private dressing room, but the furniture was familiar. He had the same desk, chair, and lighting trucked to every arena where UCW had a show. It was a personal extravagance in a man otherwise occupied by the bottom line, and I often wondered why he did it. There was a part of Malone that seemed to crave stability amid the chaos of the wrestling life. The desktop didn't hold much: Malone's cell phone, a portable printer, and a copy of that night's booking sheet and script for the show, with a list of matches and referees, and the agents who were responsible for each match.

"All right, Digger's not your problem. His mouth caught up with him. I knew that would happen. You walk around that size, you get used to people being very careful around you."

"He should've been more careful of me," I said.

Tomlinson nodded. He opened the middle drawer of the desk and drew out an electric shaver. He flicked the button, and it buzzed to life. I watched him shave. He did it unconsciously, the way some people played with cards or coins. He didn't need to shave; it was just something to do with his hands.

"You're right. But you need to watch out for Digger. He's got some stroke around here, you understand?"

"Malone, I'm not going to be around long enough for it to matter. So what the hell? Let him be pissed off. He got knocked on his ass. It'll probably be good for him."

Malone shut the shaver off and put it down. He took a deep breath in and then grinned at me.

"I don't intimidate you a whole hell of a lot, do I?"

He never had. I had made a lot of money in the wrestling business before I ever went to work for Malone Tomlinson. By the time UCW signed me to my final deal, I was already preparing to bail out. That three-year contract just added another layer to the parachute.

"All I'm here to do is find out who killed Ray," I said.

"I can't have you starting fights with my wrestlers, you know that."

"That wasn't a fight," I said.

"What the hell was it, then?"

"Just, you know, a conversation that got out of hand."

Malone grinned, blinking it on and off like a caution light. There was nothing for me to say. I had no plan past getting my hands around the throat of whoever had done for my friend.

"All right, but look, do me a favor: Apologize to him. Make nice, so that he'll be a little bit easier to deal with. You know how this works. My God, you saw how Ray navigated the locker room all those years."

He was right about that. Ray was a much better backstage politician than me. I thought about it for a minute, decided it wouldn't cost me anything to try to make nice with Marcus Digger.

"Fine," I said. "As a favor to you."

Malone picked up the shaver and turned it on again. He put the head to his face and began rubbing away at his nonexistent beard.

"Thanks, Donovan. I owe you one."

Malone picked up his phone and made a call. Within two minutes, a soft, respectful knock sounded at the door.

"Come," Malone said, and Marcus Digger came in. Behind him, Mike Austin loomed in the doorway. Austin saw me, hesitated, and then stepped into the temporary office. I stood up, my left leg a little in front of my right, my hands coming up above my waist. I was ready to fight again.

"What the fuck," I said. Digger stared at me. His eyes were puffy where he'd been crying, and his lip was so swollen that I doubted he could cut the promo Malone wanted that night. But I wasn't really concerned with Digger at that moment. Mike Austin was the problem, and I was already starting toward him when he held both hands up, palms out.

"I don't want any trouble with you," Austin said. "What's past is past, man. Leave it."

Mike Austin had the goddamned audacity to say that to me. Austin, who had politicked against me, who had wanted me out of the way to advance his own career, whose chief duty was to stooge on his so-called friends in the locker room, wanted to let things go. I'd nearly let Ray kill him a long time ago, and sometimes I wished I had.

I stopped. My blood beat loudly at my temples, and I had to take several breaths to get myself back under control. I had to remember that I was a guest here. I wasn't employed by UCW or Malone Tomlinson anymore. If I went off again, I ran the risk of getting thrown out of the building. I couldn't afford that. I knew deep down that whoever had killed Ray was connected with UCW. All I wanted to do was find the killer and make them pay.

Austin put his hand out to me. The goddamn nerve of the man. His face held nothing back, though. He was being sincere. I touched his fingertips with mine. We were both old-school enough that neither of us applied any pressure. Mike and I locked eyes, and he nodded at me once.

"Fuck-all if this ain't old home week," Digger said. "If you two assholes are done eye-fucking each other, can we get on with whatever this is?"

He leaned his ass against Malone's desk and folded his arms across his chest. I took a deep breath.

"I shouldn't have hit you," I said. "I lost my best friend this morning, and I'm feeling the strain. I apologize."

"Go fuck yourself," Digger said, shoving off the desk and walking toward me. I was ready to drop him again, but this time Austin stepped between us before anything could happen. By then, Malone was out of his seat and around the desk. He interposed himself between Digger and Austin, making sure that there was too much space between us to swing effectively.

"Stop it," Malone said. He was an old man, in his seventies at least, but his frame was wide and the years of work he'd put in at the gym had left him heavily muscled. "I asked Donovan to apologize to you, and he did it like a goddamn man. What the hell is wrong with you?"

I relaxed. Malone and Austin were between Digger and me, so nothing was going to happen. Malone straightened and walked back around his desk. Austin maintained his spot between Digger and me.

"Sit down," Malone said, motioning to the chair where I'd been sitting. His eyes were boring a hole in Digger's forehead. The big wrestler sat. If Malone Tomlinson had told him to roll over or fetch, he would have done that, too.

"You're mad because he messed up your face, but he could have taken your eye. He could have tied you up and made you shit yourself on national TV, Marcus."

"He ain't that tough," Digger said. "He's a washed up old man."

"He is that tough," This time it was Austin that spoke. "He is a badass, and I know firsthand. He put you down once, like you were a child. This old, outta shape man wiped the mat with you."

The air in the room felt very still. Malone took a deep breath, held it, and blew it out. His hair was freshly barbered, and his gray summer-weight suit was custom-made. Malone Tomlinson was in complete control, and he wanted us to know it.

"I asked Donovan to apologize to you, a personal favor to me," he said. "He did it, because he's a man of his word. Now it's your turn."

"You're asking me to apologize to this asshole?"

"No, I'm telling you to. Ray Wilder was a legend in this business, no matter what you thought of him personally. Insulting him to one of his best friends was wrong. I think you know that."

Malone reclined his chair all the way to its limit and put his feet back up on his desk. "Go ahead. Whenever you're ready."

Digger shot up from his seat like a beanstalk growing to the clouds.

"The hell I will," he said. He looked around at me. "I don't have anything to apologize for."

"You'll do what I told you to do," Malone said. He didn't move, didn't even look up at Digger's outburst. His voice was quiet, but it carried the weight of authority. Digger hung his head. That's the moment we all knew he was going to apologize. It was just a question of how long it would take. Malone looked down at the script on his desk and started to read. He took a red felt-tip pen from his jacket and began to mark up the script with edits that would eventually work their way into that night's show.

After a while, Digger lifted his head.

"I apologize," he said. Malone never looked up from his work. Digger turned on his heel, brushed past Austin, and went into the hallway. He left the door open behind him.

"That was fun," Austin murmured. I'm not sure Malone even heard him. The matter was closed as far as he was concerned. Austin and I looked askance at one another. I finally shrugged and followed Digger out the door.

The area was empty, which was fairly normal for that time of day. As things picked up near showtime, the hallway near Malone's office would become more crowded with writers and producers and agents. Wrestlers politicking for different finishes or pitching ideas to get themselves over would be jostling with ex-screenwriters who were too young to know that they shouldn't be taken seriously. But right now it was just me and the guy who'd been my worst enemy when I retired.

"You ain't gonna believe me," Austin said, "but I'm sorry as hell about Ray."

I didn't say anything for a minute, just let the silence hang between us.

"I believe you," I said, finally.

"You wanna go talk about it?"

Turns out, I did.

EIGHT

RAY AND I were old. That's what it boiled down to, Mike Austin told everyone. Yeah, we were still in the mix for the tag team titles, but that was only because I could still move, could still *go*, as we called it. Ray was the elder statesman, and ever since Malone Tomlinson exposed the business, telling everyone that what we did was predetermined and the outcomes fixed, the fans had recognized Ray for the physical genius he was. We couldn't get them to boo us anymore, so we were babyfaces by default. He'd hang out on the ring apron and wait for the hot tag. He'd come in like a house on fire, chopping and punching and backdropping the heels, and then do a little sequence that led directly to the finish.

It was easy work, and we could've gotten away with it for another five years. Mike Austin couldn't see it, though. He was a Canadian wrestler who had worked in the shadow of guys like Ray for almost the entirety of his career. His matches were clinics. Everything looked good, and Ray had even helped make him as a main eventer a few years before, dropping the world title to him after the final singles run of his career.

That wasn't enough for Austin, though. While he had strong

49

feuds with guys like Roland Gunner and Billy "Excitable Boy" Page, the TV ratings didn't lie. The Neilsen ratings were broken down into fifteen-minute increments, and our segments as a tag team were some of the highest-rated quarter-hours on UCW programming. Even if he was declining as an in-ring talent, Ray could still talk people into the building with his flamboyant promos.

"I don't care if they know the whole goddamn game is fixed," Ray said one time when we were sitting at a booth in the Cheetah Club and watching the dancers strut their stuff along the neon catwalk. "They can think everything else in the business is fake. But when they see us, I want them to know that we are by-God real."

I agreed with him. I always agreed with Ray, which was one of the reasons we stayed friends. He was a perennial world champion, always near the top of the card. A lot of people say that I rode his coattails, and maybe I did. But I also gave him ten more years in the business. He had someone who could do the heavy lifting in the ring, and who could watch his back outside of it.

The funny thing with Mike Austin was that he and Ray looked at the business in a similar manner. Austin's in-ring work was among the best of his era. He was tough, and he had credibility with the fans and support in the locker room. The reason he disliked Ray was simple: He wanted to be the man. As long as Ray was on the card and pulling in viewers, no one fully believed that Austin could carry the company.

That night at the Georgia Dome, Ray and I dropped the tag titles to Rusty Shelton and Baby Barnes, a couple of Austin's henchmen. It didn't make any sense, because we weren't in any kind of a program with Rusty and Baby. They were a couple of journeymen wrestlers who just happened to be in Mike Austin's clique, so we figured that Austin was politicking behind the scenes. That was fine … everybody does it, and we knew we'd get our win back sooner or later. It didn't matter, except that Austin was exercising some backstage power, showing off that he had a little stroke.

He wouldn't come straight at us. That was another part of it.

Austin was a second-generation wrestler whose father had been a major star and then a promoter in western Canada. There was no denying that Austin was tough as nails, that he'd come up in the last vestiges of the territory system in a remote area that bred tough, hard people. Usually the Canucks we knew were straight-forward—unless they were from Montreal, an area that seemed to constantly produce wrestlers predisposed to subterfuge in the locker room and in the ring—and we treated them accordingly.

But Austin was different. Shortly after Ray dropped the strap to him, he went on a Canadian talk show and badmouthed Ray. Now, a lot of that is normal. You talk shit about someone to build up a rivalry, or to promote a specific match. But we'd had a long meeting before Ray agreed to lose the title to Austin. The Wild Child knew that he was at the end of his last real big-money run, and he wanted to "do the honors," for Austin in a way that would set him up to be the next dominant champion. Ray made a hand-shake agreement that night: He was out of the world title picture for good. Instead, Ray and I would run with the tag team division, working some of the younger guys and getting them ready for spots further up the card.

We'd all left the meeting feeling good about it. Or so we thought. Then Austin goes on this Canadian talk show and tears down Ray, and clips of the interview begin circulating the next day. Malone made sure Ray saw it before arriving at the locker room.

"So you defeated Ray Wilder for the title," the interviewer says. "That must feel incredible, the pinnacle of your career."

"Oh, I'm glad to finally have the belt," Mike Austin says. He's sitting on the interview set with the title propped in his lap so that the viewers can get a good look at it. The message is clear: There's a new sheriff in town. "I have to say that wrestling Ray wasn't everything I had hoped for. He's pretty washed up now, you know."

The interviewer pauses for a moment, seemingly gathering her thoughts. This was an answer that she didn't seem prepared for.

"It took you forty minutes to beat a washed-up wrestler?" She asks sweetly, slipping a little poison dart in there. Austin felt it, too.

"Well, uh, I mean, that's how they booked it," Austin said. "You have to give the fans their money's worth, so I had to carry him for a good long while there."

"I see," the interviewer says. "What's next for you?"

It went on that way for a while. Austin would talk about upcoming opponents, but over the course of the half-hour talk, it was clear that he was holding a grudge against Ray and put him down at every opportunity. A has-been. A nothing. An old man.

Ray, of course, was beyond furious.

"That limp-dick piece of shit never saw the day he could carry me," Ray said. He slammed the laptop shut and threw it against the wall. It scarred the tan-painted sheetrock, and the machine shattered when it rebounded and hit the floor. Ray picked it up as if it were hot and went to the balcony. We were on the sixth floor of the Marriot. I was half bombed from a tray of gin and tonics, while Ray was up on whatever the fuck he was on that day. He threw the laptop off the balcony, flinging it like a frisbee. For a long moment, there was no sound at all. Far below, we heard a faint splash as the laptop hit the pool.

"You gotta calm down," I told him.

"Calm down? Goddamn it, Alex. I'm gonna take his fucking eye out the next time I see him. Let him explain it to Malone."

Back when I broke in, the babyfaces and the heels stayed at different hotels. Not anymore. Now Ray and I were on the fourth floor of the Hilton. Austin was on the tenth. We went up the emergency stairwell instead of using the elevator, because there were no cameras in the stairwell. Ray was taking the steps two at a time, and I wasn't far behind him. At the entrance to the tenth floor, Ray paused to catch his breath. I was glad, because it gave me a chance to puke on the ninth floor landing.

The next thing I knew, Ray and I were on either side of Austin's door, pressed against the wall like we were riot cops about to bust in for an arrest. Ray banged his heavy, hard fist against the door and dropped his voice an octave.

"Room service."

After a moment, the door opened a crack. When it did, I rammed my shoulder hard against it and we boiled in. Austin had come to the door draped in nothing but a towel. Ray punched him in the nose, a good right hand with a lot of power behind it, and Austin went down. He struggled to get up as I closed and locked the door behind us.

"What the fuck, Ray?" Austin was holding his nose with both hands, and his towel had dropped away. His nose was bent at an unnatural angle.

The Wild Child hit him again, a left hand about an inch below the navel. Austin's air came out in a great rush, and when he bent over Ray twisted his fingers into Austin's hair and began to drag him to the balcony.

The room was mostly, but there was a shape on the bed that hadn't moved since we came in. I flicked on a light, and the room came into sharp focus. Baby Barnes was in the bed, covers pulled up over his stomach. His eyes were very big.

"Ray," I said.

The Wild Child saw, but he was intent on Austin.

"Keep him there," he said. "I'm gonna deal with what's on my plate." He kept his hand tightly wound in Austin's long, stringy hair. The sliding glass door to the balcony was unlocked, and Ray dragged Austin through. I had no doubt that Ray was going to throw the new champion off of the tenth floor balcony.

Baby Barnes and I just looked at one another. Maybe I was in shock. I hadn't suspected that Austin went that way, but I on the other hand, It didn't surprise me. Barnes had been out, and aggressively so, about his sexuality since he broke into the business a few years before. He thought of himself as breaking barriers for the LGBTQ community, and maybe he was. But it also made him a pain in the ass to deal with sometimes.

"We can't let him kill him," Barnes said. "Please."

I didn't say anything. On the balcony, Ray and Austin were struggling hard. I could see their silhouettes against the glass, elongated arms and torsos, flickering shadows against the steady antiseptic light of the room. They made very little noise.

"I'm getting dressed."

I didn't make a move to stop him. Baby slipped into Zubaz workout pants and a long-sleeved T-shirt that advertised the Gay 90s, an LGBTQ-friendly bar in Minneapolis. By the time we went out, Ray had Austin on his back on the freezing-cold concrete, hands tight around the man's throat. Austin was flailing, alternately struggling against Ray's hands or reaching for the Wild Child's face. The new champ's face was turning blue.

"Help me," Baby said, shoving past me. I followed him, and we each got hold of one of Ray's arms. The muscles were corded, hard. The pressure on Austin's throat must have been tremendous. We eventually pried Ray off of the man and pulled him back inside. Austin rolled over and began to retch, strings of saliva running from his mouth to the balcony floor.

Ray turned on me, slapping my hands away. He grabbed the front of my shirt and shoved me against the wall. I raised my hands, palms out. I wasn't going to fight Ray Wilder in the middle of someone else's hotel room.

"You're supposed to have my back," Ray said. "You don't take the side of these fucking queens."

Baby Barnes had returned to the balcony and was trying to help Austin inside, with only moderate success. When he saw that Ray had turned on me like a rabid animal, he hurried over and slipped an arm under Ray's chin. He used his other arm as a lever and applied a rear naked choke—what we'd call a sleeper hold in wrestling. It's one of those legitimate moves that wrestling has co-opted. It can be easily faked, or "worked," but if you need to put someone out with it, it's incredibly effective.

Baby clamped down with the pressure, and Ray was out on the

carpet in less than ten seconds. As soon as he felt Ray go limp, he released the hold or else Ray might have been seriously injured. Instead, the Wild Child swam back to consciousness within thirty seconds or so. He stared wide-eyed at the room around us, as if he'd never seen it before.

"The thing he doesn't understand is that you were helping him," Baby said. He'd returned to Mike Austin now, kneeling by the man's head. "Keeping him out of prison is helping him."

It says something about the wrestling business that none of us ever thought about calling the cops. But as long as Mike didn't actually die, we weren't going to involve the authorities. Wrestling handled its own business, and whatever went down between Ray and Austin would stay between them. It's why Malone made sure Ray saw the clip before he came to the building; it was his way of keeping everything professional inside the locker room. As long as they hashed out their personal stuff away from UCW events, Malone didn't care.

It was the beginning of the end for me, although I didn't know it at the time. I'd retire within a few years, and eventually Austin would come out of the closet and admit to his relationship with Big Baby. But he always kept his thumb on Ray and me. We never got the kind of momentum we had before Austin's first title reign, and any time one of our programs started getting more heat than the main events, he'd try to bring us down from a red-hot boil to a simmer.

Ray never forgave him for that, and neither did I.

NINE

MIKE WAS OLDER and grayer than I remembered. Once he had retired and taken an office position for Malone, he'd embraced the corporate lifestyle. He wore a button-down shirt with a paisley tie and tan chinos carefully ironed and creased. He'd cut his hair, and now he looked mostly like a mid-level insurance executive. At some point he must have come off the juice, because he was maybe eighty pounds lighter than when he'd been wrestling. His shoulders weren't as rounded, and his chest wasn't as thick. He still looked athletic, like a former high school athlete who's kept in shape.

A lot of guys in our generation used steroids, or human growth hormone, or some combination of the two. I never judged them for that. Everyone was looking for an edge. I didn't use them, because I had pretty good size anyway. My trouble was keeping my weight down. Truth to tell, it still is.

"I'm sorry about Ray," Austin said.

I scrubbed my face with my palms. The few hours of sleep that I'd gotten weren't enough. I felt like I was running on fumes.

"You and Ray real good friends lately?" I asked. "He never mentioned it to me."

Austin paused, looking down the dark hallway.

"Not friends. Not enemies, either. Ray was complicated, man, you know that. There's a lot of people who liked him, but hardly anybody trusted him."

I could see that. Wrestling was always a me-first business. You were the attraction, the commodity, so you had to look out for yourself. Nobody else would. It's the way wrestling had been for decades, from Gotch and Hackenschmidt to the Funks and Brisco, all the way up to the so-called "Attitude Era" of the mid-1990s. It was at that point that promoters like Malone Tomlinson realized that they could capitalize on the company name, make the promotion itself the star of the show. Wrestlers name-dropped the promotion in every interview. UCW had become the ubiquitous name brand, like Kleenex, and the stars in the wrestling sky had become dimmer.

This had a dual purpose: It made the promotion more important than the individual wrestler, so that no one could ever become larger-than-life. Wrestlers—even guys like Ray—have a shelf-life, and once you're past your sell-by date, the promoters and bookers can't make money off of you anymore. But since no one was larger than life anymore, since no one drew big money, wrestlers' payoffs were smaller now, too. Guys like Ray and me probably seemed selfish to the younger ones. We'd made our money and had our fun during the time when the business was a home for freaks and outlaws and people who just didn't give a good goddamn. We were the last outlaws.

"Come on," Austin said. "Let's go get a cup of coffee."

Catering was all the way in the back of the locker room area, and as usual, it looked like a bomb had gone off in the middle of a smorgasbord. Wrestlers usually ate at least two meals from catering on show days. You'd grab lunch as soon as you came in, and then snag a to-go plate to eat at your hotel if there was anything left. Those to-go plates were often the target of unfunny practical jokes, so a lot of the more experienced boys took their food and hid it while they did their match.

Austin and I each grabbed a paper cup of ugly, dark brown coffee. He used milk and sweetener in his, but I drank mine black. We sat in metal folding chairs lined up against the far wall, a little space between us.

"I heard you and Baby broke it off," I said. "I'm sorry it didn't work out."

Austin ducked his head in acknowledgement. He had only come out in the last few years, and that was at Baby Barnes' insistence.

"When he quit wrestling, he quit everything," he said. "I came off the road to find almost everything I owned had disappeared. He fucking cleaned me out. And what am I gonna do, file a police report? If I ever find that little bitch again, I'm going to take it out of his hide."

I sipped some coffee. I understood what Austin was feeling all too well.

"That why you're still working for Malone?"

Austin nodded, his face mostly neutral.

"Suit and tie, show up at every card. Just like before. Only now I don't have to take the bumps." He paused. "They're mostly good kids, you know? They listen, they're coachable. Better athletes than we ever were."

That's how it goes, you know. The athletes in any sport get bigger, stronger, faster. The kids in the ring today could do things I never could, things I would never want to do. I don't think I ever came off the top rope once in my career. I didn't do flips or flying whatever-the-fucks. I didn't have to. My expertise was being in the right place at the right time, doing the right thing. That was my whole deal. Part of that was Ray's doing, I think. Riding up and down the roads with him, accompanying him on the Lear jets, drinking and eating with him almost every day for more than twenty years, he taught me how to work the crowd into a frenzy with just a look, with the way I held my shoulders or hands.

I felt like one of the last practitioners of a nearly lost art. Austin here was probably one of the few left who knew most of the things I did. He was a second-generation wrestler, had followed his father and brothers into the business. He probably knew more than I did.

"You know anybody pissed off at Ray?"

"You want a list?"

I looked at him, the hard look, the one I reserved for ugly drunks or assholes who came into the pub wanting to pick a fight.

"Yeah, all right," Austin said. "I mean, we can ask around. But Ray wasn't always popular. You know that. He rubbed a lot of people the wrong way. The boys now want to stay in their rooms and play video games. Ray wanted to be in the hotel bar, trying to get laid."

"He have trouble with anyone in particular?"

Austin thought about it, rubbed his stubbly chin.

"You know Ray."

I barked a harsh laugh.

"Yeah," I said. "That's the problem."

Austin waved his arm in front of us, like a teacher wiping a difficult math problem from a blackboard. I finished the last of my coffee.

"He was having money trouble, too, I think."

"Ray? Money trouble? I'm shocked, shocked I tell you."

Austin and I shared a smile at that. I don't know what he was remembering, but I remembered the Ray Wilder who bought drinks for the room, who bought so many custom-made suits that he ran out of space in his closets and had to store them in the garage, whose gold-rimmed sunglasses were real gold. Ray made a lot of money, but he never kept any of it. It flowed through his hands like water through a chain-link fence.

"I know he hit up some of the locker room for loans, but you know how Ray is with loans. Those kids are never gonna see that money again."

"He ever ask you?"

Austin chuckled.

"He wouldn't. Ray was how he was. We might've made peace, but we were never gonna be close. You know he sold the old ICW belt, right?"

I hadn't. That gold belt was one of a kind, handmade in Mexico. It had lasted as the representation of the world championship from the late 1960s to the mid-80s. By the time Bill Cunningham had bought out all of the other ICW promoters and tried to chase Malone on the national stage, the belt was basically falling apart, and Cunningham had a new one commissioned by Las Vegas silversmith Charles Crumrine. The dirt sheets—weekly newsletters that covered the inside stuff on wrestling, including the latest gossip—said Ray had taken the original home with him, and no one had objected.

"How much did he get for it?"

"They say a hundred grand. But that's not the problem."

I put my face into my palms and asked what the problem was.

"Ray sold it like three other times, too."

"Oh Jesus."

"Yeah," Austin said. "It was pretty bad, man. Malone stepped in and settled the debts. I don't know what the hell Ray's latest contract was, but he couldn't have been making a lot after all that happened."

I thought about it for a minute. If Ray was in bad shape financially—bad enough that he'd tried to scam a bunch of people for the old world title belt—then where was he getting his money? Austin was probably right about Ray's current contract. It certainly had to be peanuts compared to the million-dollar years in the 1980s and 1990s. Ray should've been retired, like me. He should be on a beach somewhere, with fat grandkids on his lap and a mai tai in his hand. He shouldn't be lying in a Birmingham morgue waiting for someone to claim the body. This new information changed things. Maybe he wasn't chasing the spotlight. Maybe he was just chasing money.

Shit.

"Who lent to him?" I asked.

Austin hesitated, and the parenthetical lines that bracketed his mouth from nose to chin deepened.

"Maybe you need to leave this to the cops, Donovan."

"The cops aren't even here," I said. "They don't know shit."

"They were here before you, man. Already came and went. Everything I've told you, they already know. You're here playing half-assed detective, but if there was anything going on here, they would've made an arrest. Wouldn't they?"

"Who lent to him?" I found myself standing, leaning over Austin. In the old days, it wouldn't have mattered. Now, he was a shell of what he had once been, physically. I could feel the old anger and menace that I'd channeled in my promos bubbling up inside me like sick poison. The hairs on my legs and arms stood on end, and needles prickled the back of my neck. I let that feeling take me away, but I kept my voice low and even. "Why don't you want to tell me?"

"Jesus," Austin breathed. He wouldn't look at me. "Start with Scotty, why don't you? I know Ray was into him for at least fifty grand."

We found Scotty at the Gorilla position, planning out camera shots with the lead producer for that night's TV show. They were deep in conversation when I grabbed Scotty by the collar and the belt loops and snatched him away. He yelped awkwardly, but by the time he registered what was happening, I propelled him toward a dark corner of the arena to chat. Behind me, I was vaguely aware that Austin stepped in to talk with the producer.

Scotty's hip hit the security bar on one of the Boutwell's interior access doors, and he yelped in pain as we went through. I kept my grip on his collar and shoved him against the far wall of the hallway we'd entered. When he turned around, I put my fore-arm hard against his throat and got right up in his face.

"When were you gonna tell me about the money?"

My voice was a harsh burst, and I was so close to Scotty that I could smell the pungent odor of pot on his breath. We were in one of the narrow hallways that ushers and vendors used in order to move around the building quickly, without navigating the crowds. It was clean and bright, but there was nothing showy back here. No marble floor, just clean concrete and cinder block walls painted flat white. Out here under the unforgiving fluores-cents, Scotty's eyes were lined and pouched, pupils dilated with a high that was rushing away like a freight train leaving town.

"Hey, come on —" he tried to say, but I pressed my forearm harder against his throat, and he gagged.

"Don't fucking lie to me, Scotty. When were you gonna tell me about the money?"

His eyes were wide with fear, and spittle trickled from one cor-ner of his mouth. His face turned red, and then Austin was next to me, pulling at my forearm, telling me to stop, that I was killing him. I took a deep breath and eased up on the pressure. Austin slid his now-slim body between us and pushed me away. Scotty kept his back to the wall, but he slid slowly down until his ass was on the floor. He made a horrible gurgling sound deep in his chest and threw up between his knees.

"Goddamn," Austin said. He moved us away from the yellow puddle, and we watched Scotty struggle to his feet. I'd known Scott Prichard a long time. Smoked dope with him more than a few times, gotten drunk together even more than that. He was one of the guys in the business that I considered a friend. If he had killed Ray, I was going to throw him off the top of the Boutwell and let the street cleaners have what was left.

"I didn't do anything," Scotty said. His voice was a ragged, dirty whisper. "I swear to God. You know me, I never hurt nobody."

"Did Ray owe you money?"

Now Scotty wouldn't look at me. He stared at the puddle of vomit at his feet.

"Answer me."

He nodded slowly.

I ran my hands through my hair. I wanted to hit something, wanted to smell blood and hear pain. I was nearly vibrating with rage and the need to punish someone. Austin kept his position between Scotty and me. He was ready to protect his co-worker, and I was eager to let him try. The way I felt, hopped up on anger and grief and too little sleep, I was ready to blow through Mike Austin like he was Kleenex. Instead, I drew in a deep breath.

"Why didn't you tell me?" I asked.

"It was between Ray and me. I didn't think it was anyone else's business."

The hallway was quiet for a long moment. There was no sound except the individual hiss of our breathing. Eventually, I had the cork back on the bottle of my rage, and I could think rationally. I didn't think Scotty had killed Ray, but I needed more information. This time when I approached him, it was more deliberate. Austin grabbed my arm as I went by, but I gave him a look. He dropped his hand, stood ready in case I went for Scotty again. Instead, I cupped Scotty's chin in my hands, almost like a lover.

"My business is what I say it is," I told him, my voice as soft and unfocused as his eyes. "Tell me what I want to know."

TEN

June 28, 1988
The Coliseum
Charlotte, North Carolina

BILL CUNNINGHAM'S FAMILY had run wrestling shows for more than fifty years. Informally, their territory was known as the Carolinas, but they controlled Virginia, West Virginia, Maryland, and occasionally parts of east Tennessee and Kentucky. Cunningham's territory was so big that he employed more wrestlers and behind-the-scenes talent than anyone not named Malone Tomlinson.

Cunningham was known as a good payoff guy, too. If you broke into the Carolinas, you were in for better money than anywhere except maybe Paul Boesch's Houston promotion. Boesch took pains to be known as the best payoff guy in the business, so coming in second to him was no small compliment as far as the locker room was concerned. The Carolinas were a difficult territory to work, though. From a travel perspective, you either had to fly in a small plane or put a lot of miles on your car.

A lot of the boys in the Carolinas owned small planes, and for a while Cunningham owned a couple eight-seaters that could fly himself and his main-eventers from town to town. But as his territory grew and he had up to three towns going every night of the week, Cunningham decided to expand further. He bought promotions in Louisiana, Oklahoma, and Kansas City. He bought Florida's booking office. While Malone Tomlinson expanded from his New York office, Cunningham was consolidating his own power south of the Mason-Dixon Line.

But he had made his moves too late. Tomlinson capitalized early, snagging top talent from around the country. Reed Ellis' American Wrestling Stars based in Minneapolis lost its top baby-face, heel, and on-screen manager in the span of six months. Pacific Coast All-Stars lost its top babyface and heel to Malone, even though they rarely appeared on TV. Mostly they were paid to stay home and never appear for the local promoter again.

It was a sea change, and most promoters were caught unaware. Eddie Graham in Florida, who had done huge box office num-bers for nearly thirty years and was one of Malone Tomlinson Senior's closest confidantes, lost everything. He killed himself, and Cunningham bought the promotion for pennies on the dollar.

But Bill had over-extended himself. He bought the promo-tions, but he was concerned that so-called 'outlaw' promotions—businesses with no financial ties to the ICW or Malone's UCW—would use the beloved local talent. So he kept them on payroll and put them on TV. He didn't do away with territory champi-onships, either, so his television programming made it seem that every wrestler had a belt.

And, of course, he loaned Ray Wilder money. Ray was Cunningham's linchpin, although almost no one outside of the business knew it. Malone had made overtures to Ray for years, hoping to get the man that nearly everyone considered the real world champion into UCW. But Ray hung in with Cunningham. It was Cunningham who had made Ray a star, who had put him in tag teams with established wrestlers and let him learn every night, who had put the microphone in his hand and allowed him the leeway to cut the kind of promos that only Ray could do, who had encouraged a dark-haired, pasty-white, nearly three-hundred pound Minnesota kid to lose seventy pounds, get a tan, and become the Wild Child he had always wanted to be.

Ray was loyal. But he was needy, too. He owned a Porsche, and he owned his own limousine, too. At some point in there, a Rolls Royce got added to the collection. Cunningham provided a driver so that after the matches, Ray could ride to the next town in style. But that wasn't enough. Ray got divorced, and his ex-wife took the house and the Rolls. As the Wild Child—as the world champion—Ray couldn't live in a dump. But his wife had taken him to the cleaners. So Cunningham bought him a house and a replacement Rolls. As the territory expanded, it was time to upgrade the air transportation. Cunningham bought a pair of jets: one for the babyfaces, and one for the heels.

The money kept flowing, but by mid-1987, it was clear to Cunningham that he was riding a dangerous wave that he could no longer control. The sea of financial burden followed him, and he began to keep a bottle of Pepto-Bismol in his bottom desk drawer. He nipped at it throughout the day, like a functional drunk trying to maintain his equilibrium.

It didn't work. The rapid expansion affected ICW's schedule, with regularly-scheduled towns getting switched to outliers in Oklahoma or Texas. Las Vegas was a frequent stop. It had been controlled, as much as it was possible to control a town like Vegas, by Reed Ellis. With Ellis out of the way, it was a free-for-all. But Cunningham had forgotten an important thing: wrestling in the Carolinas and Virginia was a way of life. There were no professional sports teams at the time. Wrestling was the show. In towns like Vegas and Dallas, wrestling was just another attraction competing for entertainment dollars.

Cunningham's promoters had to switch nights and venues for their shows to compensate for the crazy travel schedule. Fans are creatures of habit: if they were accustomed to Saturday night shows at the Coliseum in Charlotte, they didn't want to switch to the smaller Grange Hall on Mondays.

Ray was the constant, though. He could go on TV and talk people into a building. And though he had that gift of gab, repetitive booking and lower-quality opponents didn't help anything. Cunningham's ICW was dying before our eyes.

We were sitting in Ray's private dressing room in the Charlotte Coliseum one night before a show. It was rare that we hit the Coliseum anymore, but this was supposed to be a big show, a Thanksgiving night spectacular broadcast over closed-circuit TV. Boxing promoters were doing big business with closed-circuit, and Cunningham thought wrestling could be just as big.

Ray carefully wiped the world title down with a chamois cloth. When he opened his robe on camera, he wanted the gold and jewels to sparkle. His boots were already laced, kneepads sitting down around his ankles. Before he went out for his match, he'd pull them up. I was taping my wrists and thinking about what I was supposed to do that night. It was a big one for me: I was winning the U.S. title from Landry Baylor. I wasn't supposed to have the belt for long, but it would cement me as a force in the main event scene. Baylor booked the shows for Cunningham, and he was a legend. 'The All-American' looked like an out-of-shape doughboy with a blonde perm and a lisp.

"I ain't nothin' but a carpenter's son," Landry Baylor said during his promo. "You know about the other carpenter's son, and brother, you better pray to him. Because daddy when I get you in that ring, there ain't gonna be no mercy—no quarter—not one little bit, baby, from me."

Landry could talk like that, and we'd crack up. He and Ray didn't always get along, but they managed to make magic together on the microphone and in the ring. I was a solid hand by then, and Landry thought I was ready for the next step. That step included beating him for the title and then working a program against him. I was thinking about how Landry didn't look strong—he didn't look like he had a single visible muscle—and he didn't look quick. But he was both. Despite how he looked, he was an incredible athlete. I was pretty sure we were going to be the match of the night. So I was pretty far in my own head when Ray started talking.

"—maybe a little more. What do you think?"

"Huh?"

"Damn, kid, why do I keep you around?" Ray laughed and plunged his hand into the Igloo cooler we shared. He pulled out the last two beers and handed me one. We cracked them open and drank. "I said that the gravy train here ain't gonna last forever. I'm thinking about hitting Cunningham with the idea of retirement."

"Yeah? You want to retire?"

"No, but I want him to think that I'm considering it. I'm thinking of opening up a couple of gyms, but you gotta have the capital to do that."

Now, Ray made money. But most of that money went to his alimony and child support, to say nothing of the parties and toys. He was also always looking for other ways to make a dollar. At that point, I don't think he saw himself chained to wrestling for the rest of his life. He was in his mid-thirties by then, with his nose in the air to sniff out other opportunities.

"I could buy a Gold's Gym franchise, but I been thinking: Why would I wanna pay them a fee? What if I franchised myself? Wild Child's Gym. Locations in Charlotte, Atlanta, Richmond, maybe Baltimore. That's to start. Then sell the name to someone else who'll run their own place. Whaddaya think?"

It wasn't the weirdest idea I'd ever heard from Ray, and I told him so.

"I could work outta the Charlotte location maybe three days a week, drive down to Atlanta one day a week, up to Richmond one day, hit Baltimore monthly, make sure everything's running tight."

I couldn't see Ray running the little day-to-day office details of a business. It wasn't that he wasn't smart enough to do it. He was plenty smart, and a goddamn genius when it came to wrestling. But I knew that if he tried to settle down to one location for long, he'd get bored. And a bored Ray Wilder was a dangerous Ray Wilder.

"You sound like you've thought this through a good bit."

"A little bit," Ray admitted. "But it's a lot to think about. You gotta get the right location at the right price, am I right? And then you gotta buy equipment, hire staff. All that shit. It could be a headache."

"Everything's a headache when it comes down to it," I said, and drank down the last of my beer. I was feeling good. Not drunk, not even buzzed. I felt integrated, as if every part of me was a well-oiled machine, every cog and gear running smoothly. I did some deep knee-bends to warm up, then touched my toes a few times to loosen my lower back and hamstrings. I didn't want to walk out there cold.

"It'd take a lot of money," Ray said. He took out a brush and started pulling it through his shoulder-length hair. The platinum-dyed hair would shine like the moon out in the arena, reflecting the house lights. I was already losing my hair, so I didn't pay it much attention.

"How much are you thinking?"

"Between four locations? A million to get up and running, maybe a little more."

"Jesus Christ," I said, straightening up. "Why are you gonna hit Cunningham with all of that?"

Ray stopped brushing his hair and looked at me with his level, smirking gaze.

"Because I can," he said. "My contract is up in two months, yours is up in what, six?"

I did the math. He was right.

"Bill can't afford to lose either one of us. He's over-extended as it is. He loses me, he loses you. And then he'll go under. They don't have anyone groomed to take either of our spots."

I sat back down.

"I never thought of it like that."

"You're a nice guy, Donovan, you don't think like a sonofabitch. It's your weakness."

"I guess so."

"I ask him for the million, and he'll come up with it. If he doesn't, I'll go to Malone. He's been calling me every week to talk about coming in. It doesn't hurt to pick up the phone and have a conversation. Malone's got some interesting ideas he's been pitching."

I didn't often see the mercenary side of Ray Wilder. Most of the time it was drinks and women and travel and locker-room bullshit. I'd stand at the curtain and watch his matches every night. Not because I was worried about someone trying to double-cross him. I was going to school on those nights, watching a master class in professional wrestling. It wasn't just what Ray did, but it was also when he did it. His timing and reactions were perfect, and he made every wrestler he worked with look better than they were.

That night, he watched my match. When I came through the curtain with the U.S. title draped over my shoulder, he was there to congratulate me.

"Magic," he said. "You guys were magic."

"You really think so?" I was short of breath and streaming with sweat. Landry Baylor had made me earn everything I got out there, and when I covered him for the pin, he'd whispered his own congratulations to me. I put my lips near his ear and whispered "Thank you." I hightailed it to the back with the title belt held high as the Charlotte fans pelted me with paper cups, balled-up programs, and ice cubes.

"Hell yes," Ray said. "Goddamn magic. I gotta follow you two, and you guys put on a classic like that?

He grinned at me.

"Challenge accepted, baby. Wooooooohooooooo!"

I sat down in my customary seat to watch Ray and Brady Reeves go at it. Reeves was an up-and-comer who'd been booked a few weeks earlier to win an over-the-top-rope battle royal with fifteen other wrestlers, with the caveat that the winner received a world title shot. Reeves was a young kid with a lot of charisma, and he was a real draw with younger fans and women. He had survived the match, and won by eliminating Rip Rogers and me at the end.

Cunningham was hoping to create another star, but unlike with Killer Miller, he was bringing Reeves along slowly. Tonight's match with Ray was just supposed to be a tease for the fans, to show them that the kid had promise. The match went off without a hitch, and after Ray showered, he told me to go ahead to the hotel without him.

"You sure?"

"Yeah," he said. "I'm gonna go ahead and talk with Bill. After that main event, he's gonna be in a good mood. No better time than now, right?"

"I guess so."

"Go have a drink for me. I'll catch a ride with Bill."

"You sure this is a good idea, Ray? Maybe sleep on it, give it a little more thought."

Ray brushed some invisible lint away from his suit jacket, then checked the crease on his cream-colored slacks. He grinned at the mirror, then turned to me with the confidence of a timeshare salesman who knows he's got a mark on the hook.

"Hey, what's a million dollars between friends?"

I picked up my bag, which was ten pounds heavier with the U.S. title belt in it. I felt good, strong and whole. Not thirty years old yet, and marked for greatness. Landry Baylor was pushing me into main event territory, my payoff for the closed-circuit match would be somewhere near five figures, maybe a little more, and Ray was working his own angle to squeeze more dough out of Bill Cunningham.

"Be careful," I said as I turned to leave. "A million here, a million there—pretty soon it adds up to real money."

ELEVEN

RAY OWED MONEY. All right. That was no surprise, and in fact it would have been surprising if he hadn't owed anyone. If Ray made a million a year, he spent two million. That's just who he was, and guys like Scott Prichard were easy money marks for carny old bastards like Ray. He knew how to bleed you, how to make you feel good about being in the orbit of not only the world champion, but a transcendent talent, a guy who essentially changed the history of the wrestling business.

I didn't think Scotty had killed Ray. The timing didn't work. Because they'd had a pay-per-view show the night before, Scotty would have been wrapped up at the building for most of the day and night. He was one of Malone's linchpin guys, usually in charge of whatever venue the company was using. That meant that Scotty and the building manager would have to walk the venue at the end of the night to assess whether the company got its damage deposit back.

I found a dark corner of the arena and sat down to clear my head. In the center of the big room, the ring loomed under the spotlight, calling for my attention like a siren calling sailors to their doom. It was deserted now, and I felt the desire to climb back between the ropes, parting them like a willing woman's legs. The one-ring circus. Feel the slight bounce of the ring underneath my feet, just a little give to make the body slams and armdrags and backdrops slightly easier to take. Between those ropes was where I had belonged.

This was the quiet time. In Malone's office, things would be buzzing. Last-minute rewrites to the show, with management and producers politicking and plotting and planning, all trying to convince Malone that their idea was the best. The run sheet would get worked and reworked until a final hard copy was printed and handed over to Malone. He'd read it, then tear it up again and start over. It was easy to criticize UCW's television, because most of the time Malone kept everything that he wanted to do in his own head, and the writers were flying on guesswork and gumption. Writing for TV was the most thankless task at UCW. Stress ulcers and burnout ruled most days.

I was trying to let my mind go blank, look at the situation like one of those 3-D puzzles that were all the rage in the 1990s, with a pattern that could be revealed if you could manage to look past the pattern on the surface. Ray had hated those, because he'd been born with a lazy eye that had a tendency to wander if he was over-tired. Most of the time, no one ever noticed it, but it was one of the reasons that you usually saw him in those gold-rimmed aviator sunglasses. He didn't want any part of his physical image spoiled. He eventually had cosmetic surgery to fix it.

Light, quick footsteps approached, and I sat up with a start. Penny Baker was there, and now she had her face on. Long, fake lashes, bronzer, wild eyeshadow, heavy lipstick, and I don't know what else. She didn't look anything like the Penny I knew, but that was the point. She was supposed to be larger than life. It was never enough for Malone for someone to simply be a wrestler. They had to be an over-the-top personality. That's how you take a grappler and turn him into a wrestling plumber, or take a journeyman underneath talent and dress him up like a hockey goon. Malone loved that shit, and he paid enough that wrestlers would go for those outlandish gimmicks.

Penny stopped a few feet away from me, put her hands on her hips, and tilted her head.

"Were you thinking or sleeping?"

I laughed.

"I don't know," I said. "You tell me."

Penny came closer. She was already in her ring gear, a fish-net nylon body stocking over multicolored tights, with Japanese-style kick pads over collegiate wrestling shoes. Malone had her doing some kind of rip-off of Harley Quinn from the Batman comic books.

"I'm not one to judge, but which one includes snoring?"

She put her elbow on my shoulder and rested her chin in her palm.

"You caught me," I said. "I came down here to think, but I'm too old to do it in one spot for very long."

"It catches up with all of us, babe."

"Well, maybe not you."

Penny straightened up, threw me a sideways grin, and twirled so that I could see her costume reflect the dim arena lights.

"You got that right, sugar. Penny Baker, eternal sunshine girl. The bad Penny who always turns up. While the boys are fighting it out up top, us little girls are down here surviving."

She paused, thinking something over.

"You're really trying to figure out who killed Ray?"

I nodded.

"I never understood why you were so loyal to him," she said. "I know what he got out of it, a permanent wingman. But you know down deep that Ray would have cut you loose if it would've helped him."

"Hey," I said. "He was my friend, Penny."

"I know, I know. But you could've done better, a lot better."

Penny took me by the arm with her hard, strong little hand and dragged me to my feet. "Come with me. Maybe it's time you learned something."

The women's locker room was on the second floor, up a narrow, rickety flight of stairs. I had to turn sideways at the landing to follow Penny. She paused and knocked twice at a door with a temporary sign that read QUEENS OF THE RING. After that, she opened the door and stuck her head inside. "Ladies, we got a guest of the male persuasion. You got any bits you don't want him to see, cover 'em up now."

A small flurry of sound grew louder when Penny swung the door open. She went in, and I followed.

"Oh my god," Katherine Ash screamed, and leaped to hug me. I hadn't seen her since I'd retired, and I hugged her back, hard. "You're really here. It's good to see you. Penny told us why you came."

Penny and Kat introduced me around. Lara, Samantha, Shalondra, Kim, and several others whose names I didn't catch right off the bat. When I'd been a full-time wrestler, the women had mostly been special attractions, and there were fewer of them. Now they had their own division, and there were many more of them. They were still second-class citizens in a lot of ways. The men had a locker room that was three times the size of this one, with room to spread out. The women's dressing room was cramped, with everyone jostling for space. Along one wall there was a long mirror surrounded by light bulbs so that they could see how their makeup looked from any angle.

Most of the women were scantily dressed. Some of that was for TV, but it looked like Penny and I had interrupted several of them in the middle of a wardrobe change. Maintaining eye contact was a challenge, but I managed. Women notice that kind of thing, and they really notice it when they feel vulnerable, like when they're half-dressed.

"You've all heard about Ray Wilder," I said. "He was shot at my bar. I—I was with him when he died."

"How awful," Kat said. She reached over and patted my arm.

The tall, lithe brunette named Lara turned away from me and began slipping out of her top. She had no tan lines, and the intricate, strong muscles in her back were revealed in sharp relief thanks to the high-watt bulbs along the mirror. I realized that I was on the verge of staring and looked away while she shrugged into a sports bra.

"I think he was killed because of something to do with his work here," I said. "Or by someone here. I want to find out who did it, and I want to know why."

Kat let her hand fall away from my arm and moved to the mirror, where she checked her makeup. Her eyes were large, expressive. She looked like she was about to cry. I hoped I was wrong about that. I'd known Kat for almost as long as I'd known Penny, and if she broke into tears, I was just tired enough and brittle enough that I might join her.

"Why should we talk to you?" The speaker was a woman in her mid-twenties who had introduced herself as Kim. She was blonde and willowy, maybe five-eight. A little too short to be a runway model, maybe, but she was still gorgeous enough to stop a man in his tracks and turn at least part of him to stone. Her ring gear was a pair of booty shorts over flesh-colored tights, with a halter top that showed a lot of exquisitely sculpted abdominal muscles. She looked fierce, ready to fight, and I could easily imagine her as an Amazon princess.

"I told him we would," Penny said. "Kim, please. He's not like Ray."

"Sure," Kim said. Like Lara, she turned away from me and began digging for something in her bag.

I looked at Penny, my eyebrows raised. I didn't understand what was going on.

Lara crossed her arms over her chest and glared at me. At first, I thought she was smirking until I realized that I'd seen that look before. It wasn't a smirk. It was rage.

"What did Ray do?"

I spoke the words softly, but everyone heard me. The room was too small to do otherwise. I looked at Kat's reflection. Her shoulders trembled.

"You expect us to believe that you don't know?" Kim hissed, spinning back to me. "Really?"

I put my hands up in surrender.

"I have no idea what's going on," I said. "Smarten me up. Please."

From her position by the mirror, Kat spoke quietly.

"Penny, can you give us a minute alone with Alex? Please."

Penny didn't look too happy about that, but she backed out of the locker room. Now I was alone with a group of women that I didn't know. A sense of otherness, a sense of I-don't-belong-in-here nearly overwhelmed me. I leaned against the counter where a dozen makeup bags sat ready to use and waited as Kat took a deep breath.

"Ray was a predator. He sexually assaulted almost every woman in this locker room."

I started to shake my head, to say no he wasn't, to tell her that I had known the man for far too long—and far too intimately—to believe her. But women know a lot of things that men don't. They see another side of us, a side we often keep closed off from other men. So I kept my mouth shut, which is a technique I should use more often. She didn't need me to judge what she was saying, she needed me to hear her.

"Tell me," I said. "I want to know everything."

Kat wouldn't look at me.

"You know why I sent Penny out, she doesn't like to hear me talk about him."

Once, when Penny and Kat were on the outs, Ray had put the moves on Kat. It hadn't meant a thing to him that the two had been an openly lesbian couple. Ray liked women, and he was used to charming his way into a woman's pants. They'd been hot and heavy for a few weeks, as I recalled. Ray even left his wife and moved into the Four Seasons for a while. Kat broke it off when she and Penny got back together. He hadn't told me a lot about it, but I could tell that he'd been genuinely hurt when Kat left.

"You know how Ray is, he's under contract, but he comes and goes. I swear, only he and Malone ever know his schedule. So one night in Portland, Ray shows up and he's talking about how this used to be Don Owen's town, telling us stories about Rip Oliver and Billy Jack Haynes. You know, giving us the good-old-days stories."

I couldn't help but smile at that. I could see Ray half-drunk telling tales of things that might—or might not—have happened. I also noticed that Kat still talked about Ray in the present tense. His murder had yet to really register.

"So a bunch of us go out with him to this creaky old bar, just an absolute dive. I mean it was only held together by layers of dirt. Ray walks in and everyone knows him, everyone's calling him champ, he's acting like he's in the middle of the Ritz bar. We close the place down, a bunch of us stumbling out to our cars, driving back to the hotel on this deserted road that's crooked as a dog's hind leg. It's amazing nobody got killed."

Kat paused, realized what she'd said. Her fingers shot to her mouth to cover the embarrassed O of her lips.

"I'm sorry, Alex," she said. "I didn't think."

"It's all right," I said. "Tell it however you need to tell it."

Out of the corner of my eye, I could see Lara leaning against the wall, with her arms crossed over her chest. She was still angry, but I thought her expression had thawed a little. I didn't want to risk a look at her, though. I was trying to concentrate on what Kat was telling me, trying to keep my reactions to a minimum. I wanted to hear what she had to say, and I needed her to keep talking. She smiled uncertainly at me, nodded to herself, and took a deep breath.

"I was barely able to walk by the time we got back to the hotel. I mean, I was absolutely blotto. You ever been so drunk that you think you have to keep drinking because you know how bad the crash is going to be? That's where I was. I wanted another drink, and Ray said he had a bottle in his room. Which, of course he did. He always does.

"So I went with him, and we had a drink. He reaches over and takes the empty glass from my hand, and when he does that, he just kind of leans in and kisses me, you know like it's a real smooth move, the Ray Wilder special … it didn't shock me, I mean I've been kissed before. Hell, I've kissed Ray before. But I told him that I didn't want that, that we were done with that part of our relationship, that Penny would be mad if she found out. Ray didn't care. He kissed me again, and just kept leaning in until I was on my back. H-he didn't stop until he was done."

Now tears did spill from Kat's eyes. They ran down her cheeks and spoiled the heavy TV makeup that she'd applied so carefully. I closed my eyes and put my head in my hands, scrubbed my face with calloused palms. I wanted to reach out to Kat, to pull her into my arms and tell her that I was sorry. Sorry for what Ray had done. Sorry for being his friend.

"What happened then?"

Kat sniffed, and wiped at her tears. Someone, I think it was Samantha, handed her a box of tissues, and she blew her nose.

"I tried to leave, go back to my room. Ray wouldn't let me. He pulled me back to the bed and made me lie down. He fell asleep, and I just lay there."

"Why didn't you leave then?"

"I don't know," Kat said. "I mean, it's not like it was the first time I'd ever had sex with Ray, so I just … accepted it. Accepted that it had happened. I laid there a long time thinking about it, going 'well, at least that's over' before I finally went to sleep."

She took a deep breath and told the rest in a rush.

"When I woke up, Ray was on top of me, inside me. And it didn't seem like there was anything else I could do. I was just there. A thing. I don't even think I was human to him at that point."

"Jesus Christ," I said. "Kat. I didn't know."

I couldn't move toward her, although I wanted to. She cleaned up her face and began re-applying her makeup, staring carefully into the mirror.

"We all have stories like that about Ray," Lara said. Every woman there had a story like Kat's, and I listened to them all. Ray used booze or weed or GHB to lay each one of them down, to assault them, to hurt them. It was impossible to disbelieve them. Lara watched me carefully, noting with satisfaction how hard each new revelation hit me. I was trying not to react, but it was like being in a street fight. Blows were landing from all directions, and I didn't know where the next one was coming from.

"I don't understand," I said. "Why didn't you tell anyone?"

There was silence in the room. Kat answered me as gently as she could.

"It's always he-said, she-said. Come on, you know that. And getting the cops involved could be … adverse to our careers. Malone made sure we knew that."

My head snapped around. "Malone knew? Why the fuck didn't he do something?"

"You don't get it," Kim said. "Ray's a star. He's been a star for forty years, Alex. He built his name on being the playboy, the one all the guys want to be and all the girls want to be with. His segments still pull some of the highest ratings on the show, and he doesn't even wrestle anymore."

I didn't want to believe it. It hurt too much to know that I had been so wrong about Ray.

Shalondra was a tiny Black woman with silvery-blue hair, the youngest of the group. Like all of the rest of the Queens, she was drop-dead gorgeous, but she was merciless as she struck the knockout blow.

"I had it written into my contract that Ray is never allowed to be alone in the same room with me," she said. "It was the only sure way I knew to keep it from happening again and keep my job."

TWELVE

August 23, 1987
The Cow Palace
San Francisco, California

THE COP SITTING across the table from me said her name was Gonzalez. She could have passed for a wrestler herself, wide and muscular, with an air of confidence that bordered on arrogance. Her hair was pulled back in a high ponytail, and she wore little, if any, makeup. Her hands looked strong, and her fingernails gleamed with clear polish in the dim overhead light. She wore chinos, thick-soled black cop shoes, a gray sportcoat with a faint weave, and a mannish Oxford button-down shirt open at the throat. Her badge was in a leather holder clipped jauntily to her lapel. Underneath her folded hands sat a buff-colored folder stacked thick with paper. Another cop, this one in uniform, stood by the door. He looked asleep.

"Thank you for meeting with me, Mr. Donovan," I know this is probably a little unusual for you, but I need your help investigating an incident that happened last night at the Gangway. You were there last night, I believe?"

I told her yes, and watched her nod in satisfaction, as if she were ticking something off of a checklist. This was a new experience for me. Usually my interactions with cops were limited to brief moments before the matches. Off-duty or auxiliary officers usually acted as security for most shows, so I tried to make nice with them beforehand, in order to hopefully ingratiate myself with them. When I was about to infuriate a whole lot of low-level, potentially violent rednecks, it was always a good idea to have the cops on my side.

I had a feeling that I wouldn't be successful getting Gonzales to like me very much. That was all right, though. I didn't really appreciate being pulled into this side room two hours before I was supposed to go into the ring. I hadn't even changed into my gear yet.

"Your real name is Alex Donovan? It's not a stage name?"

"No, it's—I mean, no. It's not a stage name. It's my real name."

Gonzales nodded again, but I realized that she wasn't nodding in agreement. It was an unconscious way of recording a fact she already knew.

"Performers in your line of work often use false names, though, yes?"

"Some do, I guess."

"But not you. Why is that?"

I didn't know what to say. Gonzales didn't help me, either. She sat there as patient and silent as one of the stone heads on Easter Island. Finally I raised my hands in surrender.

"I don't know how to be anyone else," I said. "I'm just a guy who wrestles. It's my job. You don't see a lot of plumbers change their names, do you?"

Gonzales gifted me with a real smile, and for a moment I saw the attractive person she must have been when she wasn't dressed for work.

"You do not," she said. "Is that what you are in wrestling? A plumber?"

Technically, the term would be a mechanic, but I wasn't going to say that to Gonzales. Mechanic was one of those inside terms that we never used around people who weren't in the business. It meant I was a guy who could be depended on to do any number of things. I knew how to work, how to position myself to help my opponent, and how to make anything that happened in the ring get over with the audience. A mechanic knows how to make things work, pure and simple.

"That's close enough for government work."

"Yes," she said, picking up the folder from the desk and opening it. She held it so that I couldn't see anything in it. "I suppose it is. Do you personally know anyone who uses a stage name?"

"Maybe. I'm sure a lot of them change their names. Orville Schottenheimer wouldn't fit on a marquee too well, you know?"

"I suppose not. Do you know anyone by that name?"

"No, it was just, you know, an example."

"Of course," Gonzales said. "I understand. Do you know a woman named Melody Hallman?"

Nothing rang my chimes, and I said so.

"That's fine." Gonzales turned to a new page in the folder. "What about Richard Thomas Williamson?"

I scratched my head. "I don't think so."

Gonzales closed her folder and put it down. She moved precisely, as if she were born for no other purpose than to sit in a small room and talk to people like me. A narrow crease appeared between her eyes, highlighting an old scar near her right eyebrow. She leaned back and crossed her arms over her chest.

"We were getting along so well. Why lie about something I can so easily check?"

"I didn't lie to you," I said. I couldn't keep the bewilderment out of my voice. "I don't know anyone by that name, and if I did, I would have said so. I don't make a habit of lying, least of all to cops."

The cop at the door snorted. The connection between Gonzales and me had become so direct, so palpable, that I'd forgotten there was anyone else in the room. She looked at the uniformed cop in her direct, unblinking manner, and he subsided without a word ever being spoken between them. When she turned back to me, the pupils of her eyes were large and black and endless. She looked like a predator trying to decide if I was prey.

"Actually, you lie to everyone, do you not? You are a professional wrestler. Your world is make-believe, like a stage magician or a circus act for children."

I didn't have anything to say to that, so I got busy saying it. Breaking into the wrestling business, I learned about kayfabe, the code that every wrestler lived by. You never acknowledged, not under any circumstance, that what we did wasn't one hundred percent legitimate. One night in Mankato, Minnesota, a fan turned the wrong way down a hallway, just looking for a bathroom. She stumbled into a curtained-off area that the boys were using for a dressing room. I was playing cribbage with Landry Baylor when I saw her come in. I yelled "Kizz-ay-fizz-abe," carny speak to alert everyone that there was a mark nearby. And then I hit Landry with the cribbage board as the locker room went nuts. Guys turned tables over in their haste to get at one another, real punches were thrown. It was ingrained in us to protect the business at all costs. By the time I dove at Landry's ankles to take him down, an usher had already taken the woman away from the locker room. She had seen us, sure, but she hadn't realized what she was seeing.

Landry had a golf-ball sized lump on his head. I had a bloody nose. A couple of the boys had loose teeth, and there were lots of scrapes and bruises to go around. But that's how things were. Even if the fan didn't know what she'd seen, we dummied up and "protected the business." We were worried that if people really knew that what we did was predetermined, that they would stop buying tickets.

Backstage, we could be ourselves: nutty, weird, funny, whatever the hell we were. I didn't realize it at the time, but that sense of fraternity isolated us and damaged our ability to function outside of a wrestling context. It's one of the reasons that the old-timers held on so long. They didn't belong anywhere else.

Gonzales leaned forward, elbows on the table, hands cupping her chin, interrupting the flow of my thoughts.

"You don't have anything to say? Do you not want to defend your honor, the —" she paused to search for a word "— the legitimacy of your business?"

I leaned back in my chair, enough to bring its front legs off the floor a little. I'd played nice, but maybe that had been a mistake. Alex Donovan was supposed to be a hard case, a guy who took no shit from anyone. To find out what Gonzales wanted with me, maybe I should stop playing her game and start being the Donovan that people saw on TV every week. My eyes narrowed, and my stomach muscles tightened. I could feel myself changing, feel the world reorient itself to the reality that I projected. I thought about the chip on my shoulder. High-school football star that no college wanted, apprentice meat-cutter at the Piggly Wiggly in Rome, Georgia. I was twenty-one years old again in my head, and fighting against being what everyone else wanted me to be. I knew that I had it in me to be somebody, but no one else saw it.

Now I was a star. I was on TV every week of the year, no reruns, no off-season. I worked my ass off every night in the ring. Sick, hurt, sad, happy. It didn't matter. None of it mattered. I outworked everyone, even Ray sometimes. And nobody could take that away from me. I wouldn't let them.

"Why don't you just tell me what you want," I said, and Gonzales leaned back a little from my intensity. It was the first human emotion I'd seen from her. I maintained eye contact with her. "Let's stop fucking around, okay?"

She broke away from my gaze, dropping her eyes to the table where the folder lay. She picked at the edges of the thing, as if she were pulling off a particularly painful scab. By making Gonzales look away from me, I'd cost her something. She was trying her best to regain her composure.

"Fine," she said, and looked from the table to me. "You know Richard Thomas Williamson. You were in the Gangway with him last night. You returned to the same hotel, where he took a young woman named Melody Hallman. She says he raped her."

"What does that have to do with me?"

"Mr. Williamson says he didn't. He says he was with you."

"I don't know anyone named Williamson," I said. "I told you that already."

"You lie."

I slammed my palms onto the table, hard. The sound echoed in the room, and the cop by the door came away from it with his hand on his sidearm. Gonzales never moved. She lifted a palm toward the cop and made a patting motion in the air, like she was telling him to go back to his post.

"Are you quite finished with the theatrics, Mr. Donovan? I know it's all a part of your act, but it's not that amusing."

"If you have something that you want to know, just fucking ask me."

"Do you know Richard Thomas Williamson?"

"No."

This time she didn't say anything when I denied it. Progress, maybe.

"Can you account for your whereabouts last night?"

"Like you said, I was in the Gangway for a while. I drank a few drinks, listened to some music. Ray was chatting up some girl."

"By Ray, you mean Richard Thomas Williamson."

The other shoe dropped, and I cursed myself for being so dense. Gonzales took in the stunned look of disbelief on my face. Ray, you asshole, what have you gotten me into here?

"You didn't know they were the same person," she said. "This man who is supposed to be your best friend."

I shook my head. If I had known, I wouldn't have been vamping around about it.

"You admit you were with him at the Gangway."

"Of course."

"What happened after that?"

"I went back to the hotel, took the room key from the desk clerk, went upstairs and caught most of The Magnificent Seven on cable."

"We can check that, you know."

I did, in fact, know that. And I didn't care. I didn't have anything to hide. I never had, but Gonzales had been so closed-off that I had no idea what she wanted. So I did what she least expected: I became an open book.

"Check whatever you like. I came back around eleven, I think —"

"The desk clerk says it was closer to ten-thirty."

I shrugged.

"Fine," I said. "I had a few drinks in my room, watched the movie. What else do you want to know?"

Gonzales pulled a photo from the folder and pushed it over to me. A young blonde woman smiled back at me, her even white teeth very bright against the dimness of the room we were in. I'd seen her the night before at the bar, talking with Ray, and I said so.

"That's Melody Hallman," the detective said. She met my eyes for a long moment. "She says she was raped by Richard Thomas Williamson."

"Call him Ray, okay?"

Gonzales frowned. "That is not his name. That's just what he uses to go out and play pretend in front of the idiots who buy a ticket to your little sham."

This time I didn't rise to her bait. She could think what she wanted to about wrestling. It was obvious that her mind was made up.

"What's Ray say about it?"

"He says he was with you. That when he and Miss Hallman got back to the hotel, she fell asleep, so he went to your room and—his words here—'put away a few.'"

I rubbed the corners of my eyes. I was very tired.

"Is that what happened?" Gonzales asked.

In that moment, I cursed Ray. I had no idea what had gone on between him and the Hallman girl. The last I'd seen of them, he was doing pretty good. She was in his lap and checking to see if Ray still had his tonsils. From what I could see, it was a very thorough check. Her dress had slid up a little, and I didn't need to pay close attention to notice she was wearing green satin panties that sure as hell didn't cover much. I caught Ray's eye when they stopped to catch a breath, shot him with my forefinger. He grinned back, and turned his face toward the girl again. I hadn't seen him since. Whatever had happened between them, something had gone wrong. I didn't know what it was, but I was seething at the idea that Ray would set me up to cover for him without a second thought. He was counting on me to think on my feet.

"Mr. Donovan," Gonzales pressed. "I'll ask again: Is that what happened?"

"It must have been," I lied. "It would explain all those empties in my hotel room."

THIRTEEN

I HAD TO get out of the building. The Boutwell is a great old building for wrestling, but for a guy like me, it's also full of ghosts. I went down the narrow staircase from the Queens' dressing room, hooked a right, and found my way to the loading bay. I passed Penny as I was leaving, waved my hand at her to let her know that I'd be back.

In the rear alley, the air felt lighter and cleaner, as if I'd shed a weighted, grimy coat once I left the building. The alley—like all alleys—was ugly and grimy and mostly empty. But it felt like paradise in that moment. Wooden loading pallets titled in an untidy stack against the back of the building, while green and clear glass glinted in the late afternoon sunlight. Gritty concrete showed oil stains, while bare black electrical cables crisscrossed overhead in layers so dense that they might have been completely random or part of some intricate pattern that I was too dumb to figure out. The place smelled like the city: Car exhaust, ancient cigarette butts, rancid Fry-O-Lator grease.

Birmingham, baby. A city on the come-up. I couldn't see it from where I was, but to the South there was the cast iron Vulcan statue, naked save for his apron in the front, his hammer at rest on the anvil near his feet. One hand held a spear tip aloft. Behind him loomed Red Mountain, with the neon WBRC letters glowing crimson. At the top of the Alabama Power building was an answering statue of the goddess Electra, gold-plated, with her fists full of lightning bolts. One side of the city ready to build, one side ready to throw down.

Around me I could feel the city pulsing. The Alabama and Lyric theatres, sitting across from one another on Third Avenue like friendly rivals. Sloss Furnace, now open to tourists, still loomed over the Eastern side of the city, a ghost of Southern steel history. Go east and find Avondale, with its brewery and some of the best hole-in-the-wall eateries in the country. I hadn't grown up here, but the place was home in a way that nowhere else ever would be.

What was I doing here? Ray had been my friend, but everything I knew about him made me angry. Was that because he had never really grown up? He'd continued to be the Wild Child all through his adult life. I was beginning to understand that Ray had really been someone without limits. He was committed to being this larger-than-life character, committed to living the gimmick. And none of us had stopped him. None of us had imposed any kind of order or discipline on him, because it was just such a goddamn good time when Ray was around.

But when I thought about what Ray had done to Kat. How he had apparently taken advantage of every woman in the locker room. And even when his behavior had become common knowledge, Malone Tomlinson had let it go on, because Ray sold tickets.

Wrestling is still a carny business in a lot of ways. It's closed off to insiders, and using agents to negotiate your contract is a rarity even in the modern age when everything is acknowledged as "fake" except for the injuries, because you don't bring outsiders in. If you smarten someone up to the way that wrestling works, you have to be selective. What matters most to people like Malone Tomlinson is your ability to put an ass in a seat every eighteen inches in the arena. While the overall wrestling attendance had never been lower, crowds still packed in for TV and major pay-per-view cards. Ray was one of the few personalities you could depend on to attract viewers and ticket sales.

Of course I knew that Ray got away with a lot. I had moved in his orbit so long that I'd gotten away with a lot, too. It got written off as 'bad behavior' or 'boys being boys.' But I'd woken up one morning and realized that I wasn't a boy anymore. I was a grown man, and I had nothing beyond a nice bank account and a body that was breaking down more every day. Flights and hotel rooms and bouncing around the ring, reacting to the crowd, making the towns, giving the fans what they wanted. What they wanted wasn't just a piece of me. It felt like they wanted everything.

We were never careful, you know? We never had to be. Because we were heels—the bad guys—the guys who did what they wanted, when they wanted to, simply because they could. Guys like Ray never turned the gimmick off. He largely did whatever he wanted to, like the time in broad daylight when he strutted down the boardwalk in Atlantic City wearing nothing but the world title belt, his Italian loafers, and a smile. Tourists were pointing, laughing. People were taking pictures. The Wild Child didn't care. When the cops showed up and cited him for public indecency, Ray took off one of his shoes, dug out the arch support to reveal his hidden cache of cash, and tried to give the man five hundred dollars to pay the fine right then and there.

He spent a night in the drunk tank, and I picked him up the next morning. Of course I did. That's what I was there for, right? Cleaning up Ray's messes. Had he ever cleaned up one of mine? I tried to think of a time when he'd been there for me the way that I'd been there for him, but I couldn't think of any. Ray was out for Ray. That was all it was about at the end of the day. It was amazing that he was still alive.

When a wrestler like Eddie Guerrero or Brian Pillman dies in a hotel room, thousands of miles away from their family, it's soul-crushing. Those kinds of guys gave every bit of their lives to the business, and it broke them. It broke their families. It's impossible to look in a mirror and not wonder if you're next.

That was where I was headed, too. I could feel it in my bones. That's why I got out. I didn't want to be one of those guys, God love them. I took the money I'd saved and built Donovan's Pub. That's where I should be right now, damn it. That was my life now, not this world of make-believe where every slight, whether real or imagined, carried so much weight.

I was loyal, sure, but I was my own man now, and I didn't owe Ray Wilder anything. The more I learned about the man he'd become—maybe even the man he'd always been—the more I realized that he was the kind of person I'd despise if it was anyone else.

I was so busy being pissed at Ray—and myself—that I didn't hear the footfall crunch behind me until it was too late. A hard boot grated on gravel, and I instinctively hunched my shoulder. It probably saved my life.

Something hard slammed into me. I took most of it on the thick trapezius muscle, but some of it caught the side of my head, too. The world turned red and went lopsided. I slewed to one side and couldn't keep my balance. I was down on the ground on my hands and knees. Everything swam around me. I could feel the side of my head swelling, pain like the birth of the world screaming in my temple. I tried to get up, but couldn't.

A length of two-by-four clattered to the pavement, and Marcus Digger stepped into the clouded corner of my vision. He kicked me in the ribs, hard, and the air rushed out of me. I rolled over onto my back. The blue sky above me, crisscrossed by the thick black power lines in geometrical shapes, could have been painted by Mondrian.

"How do you like getting suckered?" Digger asked. "Asshole."

There were a couple of others with him. I thought I recognized their faces, but I couldn't put names to them. They were just a couple of the boys, kids happy to get TV time and move around in the shadow of a star like the Gravedigger. I remembered how that felt, although empathy wasn't doing me a whole hell of a lot of good right now.

"Malone wants me to apologize? Fuck that shit. And fuck you."

They put the boots to me. I covered up, folding my arms around my head as best I could, trying to roll a little and save my kidneys from the worst of it. There's a way, in wrestling, to pull your blows. We call it "working" your punches and kicks. These guys weren't working. They were stomping and kicking full force. They wanted me to be another grease stain on the alley pavement. I want to tell you that I fought back, but I didn't. I was in survival mode, just trying to get through it.

In movies, the hero wins when the odds are stacked against him. You look at any action flick, and you see a guy taking on multiple opponents, taking them out as they conveniently attack one by one. Real life ain't that way. In real life, someone sucker punches you and you go down. If there's more than one of them, it's usually over before it starts. By the time you know you're in a fight, you're already beat to a pult. If you ever want to get back up, you'd better get back on your feet quickly. When Digger hit me with that piece of wood, it really crossed my running lights. I wasn't doing much for myself except grunting in pain.

Mike Austin and Scotty Prichard saved me. Suddenly there was space where there hadn't been before, and I rolled toward it. My head wasn't clear yet. There were staticky bursts of information coming through, like telegrams from a distant planet. I could see that Austin had one of the younger guys pinned against a wall, while Scotty had another one locked in a reverse chinlock. Scotty was on his back on the ground, with the kid on top of him. The kid was heavier, but Scotty had his legs locked around the guy's waist and was squeezing for all he was worth.

Digger paid them no attention. He came for me again, but this time when he pulled his foot back to kick me, I rolled myself into his other leg—the one that had all of his weight on it. I felt the leg flex, and Digger went down in a heap. I scrambled to my feet, and he came up limping.

I wiped blood out of my eyes. My sport coat was gone, my shirt was torn, and my body hurt everywhere. At some point, I'd lost a fingernail. I didn't care about any of that. Digger came for me again, using his weight advantage to try to bull me back against the wall of the building. He was bigger, and stronger, and younger. The longer the fight went on, the more it would turn to his advantage.

I was able to slide one of my arms over his, while the other hooked under his shoulder. He kept shoving forward, thinking that he had the advantage. I turned my hip then, and used it as a pivot point while maintaining my over-under grip. Because I had a lower center of gravity, Digger rolled over me and we hit the concrete at the same time. The difference was that all of my body weight landed on him. The air went out of him in a great guttural rush, and he tried to roll away from me.

No, none of that. I threw a leg over him, and then I was astride his torso, my hands raining down blows to his face. Now he was the one trying to cover up and not being too successful at it. My blows rained down. His nose pulped when a left hand got through, and he bucked under me, trying to get free, trying to turn and run away. He finally managed to roll over to his belly, but I moved with him and maintained my position above him. He kept squirming, so I grabbed his hair and banged his head against the pavement. And again. Now the red glare of my own pain was gone, and all that was left was rage.

Digger's hand was slapping the ground next to him, and I realized that he was tapping out. Giving up. Did he think this was a contest? He had come for me, so scared and unsure of himself that he'd had to hit me from behind and bring friends along to help. And now that it wasn't going his way, he thought he could just tap out?

While I had my hands in his hair, I ground his face against the pavement, rubbing it back and forth until blood smeared like finger paint.

Then hands were on me, pulling me, dragging me away.

"Stop it," Austin said. His voice sounded very far away. "You're killing him, Alex."

"So what?" I said.

I heard Austin tell the others to stop fucking around and help him, for God's sake. More hands grabbed me, and this time when they pulled me away I wasn't able to get back to Digger. I wanted to, though. I wanted more of his blood in the dirt, wanted my teeth on his goddamn throat. Austin finally managed to bend my arm back in a hammerlock and pushed me against the wall. We stood there, both of us trembling like Thoroughbreds after a hard race, and waited for me to calm down.

A little while later, I sat on a round vinyl stool in the Queens' dressing room. Penny Baker dabbed at my face with an alcohol swab, and I winced.

"Don't be a baby," she said, but she was smiling when she said it. "Can you come back full time? Digger needs his ass kicked every chance he gets."

I knew that she meant the remark to be lighthearted, but I didn't say anything in reply. I didn't like losing my temper. It happened so rarely that it surprised me. I was supposed to be a guy who picked his spots, who waited for the perfect moment to enact his revenge.

Maybe that wasn't me anymore.

"I don't think this is going to need stitches," Penny said. I grunted.

She took her hand away from my face, trailing her fingers gently across my skin. There was nothing erotic or electric about it. Penny was the most out-of-the-closet lesbian I'd ever met, and we had known each other for a long time. I wasn't sure how she had managed to keep so much of her soul while she gave so much of herself away every night. She was a mother hen for everyone in the locker room who was lost and alone and confused.

"What the hell happened to Ray?" I asked. "I don't mean at the end. Everywhere I turn, I find out that he's changed. He's not the man I knew."

There was a long pause while Penny worked on another one of the cuts that Digger and his minions had inflicted on my scalp. This one was far back, near the bald spot I'd had for most of my adult life. The alcohol stung, but Penny's hands were strong and sure, so I stayed as still as I could.

"Maybe he never was," she said.

"What do you mean?"

"You were always loyal, but was that loyalty ever returned? Ray would have thrown you overboard in a second if he'd needed to. You were disposable to him. We all were. He was living the gimmick, right there in the middle of the Ray Wilder show, and all we—all any of us were—were accessories in his playhouse. You need to start realizing that, Alex."

I didn't want to believe her. I'd ridden the roads with Ray, flown on the planes, drank the booze, smoked the weed, and watched his back for more than twenty years before I walked away. We had been friends, dammit. Real friends.

Hadn't we?

And then all I could think about were the times I'd gotten Ray out of a jam, the times I'd stood up for him when no one else would. I couldn't remember one single instance where he'd pulled my fat out of the fryer. Of course, I'd recently been hit in the head with a two-by-four and taken a hell of a beating from three assholes who really meant it. What the hell could I really be sure of at this point?

But in the moment, everything felt true. I had been incidental, a body to run interference, a driver, a confidante. A stooge. The guy who runs to the bar when the champ's glass is empty. He'd always called me an intimidator, an enforcer. What was I really? It was starting to look like I'd been nothing but his stooge.

FOURTEEN

April 3, 2010
Huntersville, North Carolina

THEY SAY THAT Lake Norman is North Carolina's inland sea, with five hundred and twenty miles of shoreline. Boaters and anglers and anyone out for a party heads to the lake whenever they can, especially if they don't want to be bothered by the tourists out on the eastern shore of the tarheel state. The barrier islands are gorgeous, and there's history like Kitty Hawk and the Wright Brothers to think about. But there's sunshine and water and fresh beer at Lake Norman, too. I guess it's all about what you're after.

Ray had a house on the lake in Huntersville, just north of Charlotte. He could fly in and out of Charlotte to make his bookings, or we could make the easy shot down to Atlanta if he felt like spending some time in the car. The house was massive, made of native stone and smoked glass. Three stories high and at least twenty-thousand square feet. There was a tennis court in the back next to a dazzling blue swimming pool. The rear portico overhung an outdoor kitchen with all of the bells and whistles. A fire burned cheerily in the built-in fireplace, and above that, an eighty-inch high-definition TV was mounted in a recessed spot made for just that sort of thing.

It was a party, and I was pleased that my best friend had remembered my birthday. I didn't want to think about how old I was, how maybe I was finally slowing down a little, and it looked like Ray had provided the perfect distraction for me. Huge washtubs of iced-down beer sat on the portico, and I grabbed one. Cracked it open, drank half of it in one go. There were maybe fifty people there, laughing and smiling and generally having a good time. Someone had put out wine and hard liquor on the bar in case someone developed a real thirst, and I had a feeling that before the party was over, I'd be thirsty as hell.

Ray was nowhere in sight, but I saw several people I knew, including Jackie Fulltone and Pepper Montez. They were drinking beer, too. Dandy Sullivan was drunk as a skunk already, but he was taking a turn at the big built-in grill, turning tomahawk rib-eyes and spilling beer onto them from an open can when the flames got too high.

There was music, because there always was. Hidden speakers played Jimmy Buffett, and in the chill spring air, I could certainly feel changes in my latitudes and attitudes.

It was cold for April, but a couple of insane women braved the pool. Somehow their bikini tops had gotten lost, or maybe they never had them at all.

"Hey," someone yelled. I turned around and it was Rockwell Riggs, a young kid that Ray liked to keep around because he allegedly muled snow for the older guys. Riggs was no more than five-eight, but what he lacked in height he made up for in width. His deltoids had deltoids, and if wrestling still attracted single women, he would have been up to his neck in pussy. "Rescue those steaks from Dandy, would you? He's drunker than Cooter Brown."

I got the tongs away from Dandy, got him going toward the pool, and then moved the ribeyes around a little bit. They looked fine to me. I moved them to a butcher's block carving board to cool and tossed some ears of foil-wrapped corn onto the grill.

A few minutes later, Jackie Fulltone came by to take the duties off my hands, and that was the last I saw of cooking duty for the day. I found a comfortable chair in the thin, golden sunlight, sipped absently at my beer, and watched the circus unfolding around me.

Katherine Ash was there, wearing a yellow sundress that showed off her long, coltish legs. I wasn't sure if she was there with Ray or Penny, so I kept my distance. Not to be unpleasant, you understand. But until I knew what the situation was, I didn't really want to stick my foot in my mouth. Kat, as always, seemed to be the center of attention that everyone swirled around. The only other person I'd ever known with that kind of energy was Ray, so it wasn't really a surprise that they'd hooked up.

She was, of course, younger than Ray by a significant number of years. That didn't seem to bother either of them, and it wasn't any of my business. My beer was gone, so I hauled myself out of the chair and went to get another. I had what I thought was a hell of a good idea, and slid one of the wash tubs full of ice next to the chair. I could dip in anytime I wanted for another cool one. The second beer went down easier, and I crushed the dead soldier in my hand and dropped it on the other side of the chair. Two down.

"There he is," Ray said from somewhere behind me. "Man of the hour, too sweet to be sour."I grinned and stood, turning around so quickly that I nearly lost my balance. Beside my chair, there were six dead soldiers, not two. Oops.

Ray had his arm thrown around the shoulders of a tall, slim, athletic-looking man named Diego Barnes. I'd met Diego a couple of times when he played basketball at NC State. He'd made second-team all-American and played pro ball overseas for a few years before coming home and setting himself up as a kind of half-assed sports agent. Ray was a client, and Diego had brokered a deal to have Ray's likeness and signature catchphrase played at every home game for the state's major sports program, except for Duke University athletics.

Nobody likes Duke, but that's OK, because they like themselves enough for everyone.

Anyway, the deal made Ray a lot of money—I'm sure it made Diego a good piece, too—and the kid had been pressing the Wild Child to let him handle more and more of his affairs. I stayed out of stuff like that. I was always in Ray's orbit, but I was never a star of the same magnitude as him. I understood that, and understood that even if Ray Wilder had never existed that I would not have had the level of charisma and the stomach for locker-room politics that it took to become a guy like Ray.

"Hey, it's your day, Diego, lemme show you around. You've never been out to the lake house, have you?"

The smile dropped off my face. Ray hadn't even seen me. Or if he had, he hadn't acknowledged me. I scratched at my beard as the world seemed to gain greater focus and clarity despite the six-pack I'd crushed. Around the far corner of the house, I found a battered Igloo cooler and took it back to the tub full of iced-down beer. I put as much beer into the cooler as I could and poured ice over it.

No one paid me any attention. But when had they ever?

Down near the shore, Ray had a dock with a twenty-eight-foot cruiser floating in the water beside it. He had all the toys. The boat was spotlessly white, gleaming in the cold near-liquid sunlight. I knew where he kept the keys. I'd been on the boat hundreds of times. The lines holding the boat moored were carefully coiled, everything tied down and perfect. Brown lake water bumped against the hull, and the boat rocked when I boarded her. She was a beautiful vessel. Ray had bought it in a bankruptcy sale, paying maybe ten grand for a boat that was worth at least ten times that much. I found the keys, weighed them in my hand. As a safety measure, they were attached to a buoyant, bright orange cork. I tore that away and let the keys rest in my palm for a little while.

Then I drew back and threw them as far as I could into the lake.

After that, I hopped back onto the dock and opened the little cooler. This beer tasted better than all the rest. I sat down on the dock and began to unwind the moorings that held the boat in place. When I was done with the bow, I tossed that line into the boat and moved down to the stern. Same deal. Sit. Unwind, unwind, unwind. Toss. Now the boat floated freely on the mostly calm water. It drifted back toward the dock, and I put both feet against the hull and pushed hard against the boat, like I was doing leg presses in the gym.

The boat skittered away, and I watched it go. I didn't feel anything, really. Maybe a far-off sense of satisfaction, but that was it. I cracked open another beer, and then the dock shifted underneath me as someone padded forward.

"Hey," Kat said from behind me

"Hey," I said. I didn't turn around. Instead, I watched the little Pleasurecraft drift farther away from the dock. It was maybe a hundred feet from shore now.

"Is that Ray's boat?"

I sipped from a cold can.

"Yep."

Kat laughed, a musical sound that made me smile despite my anger.

"Oh, Jesus. He's gonna be pissed."

I didn't say anything. Kat slipped off her sandals and sat beside me, letting her toes trail in the cold water. Her shoulders were freckled and muscular, and her tan looked dark and smooth against the yellow sundress.

"You enjoying the party?"

"Sure," I said. It seemed rude not to reply.

Kat reached over and patted my knee. When I looked at her, she was smiling.

"You don't lie well," she said. "Maybe that's a virtue."

I snorted.

"Not in this business," I said, casting a glance back over my shoulder at the party. "Probably why I'm twenty-something years in and still Ray's lackey. If I knew how to lie—or who to lie to—maybe I'd be the one in the main events."

From behind us there was a shout, and we turned around to see Dandy Sullivan and Rockwell Riggs struggling against one another. Riggs was small, but strong. Sullivan was one of the old hands, though. He knew what he was doing, and he currently had Riggs in a side headlock that was so tight that Riggs' shaved head was turning purple. Dandy maintained the hold, slipped his body in front of Riggs, and threw the younger man with a rolling hip-lock. When they hit the ground, all of the air went out of Riggs in a great whoosh. The fight left him at the same time.

I started to my feet, but by the time I got up, a couple of the other wrestlers had already separated them. Riggs was on his hands and knees, puking. Dandy had his hands up to show that he wasn't a threat to anyone. He was grinning from ear-to-ear. If he hadn't been drunk, Dandy might've killed the kid.

Beside me, Kat hadn't even moved. I sat down again, and we watched Ray's boat drift away toward the middle of the lake. I opened the cooler and offered her a can. She took one, opened it, and then we toasted one another.

"You know I've been living out here?" She asked.

Somewhere nearby a bass broke the water near the shore, its scales flashing in the sunlight and sending concentric rings of water rippling out endlessly.

"Ray told me you were having some trouble with Penny."

Kat rubbed at her eyes, shook her head hard as if to clear it.

"You boys have fun talking about us? Did you get all the dirty details you wanted? I could tell you some goddamn things about Penny that nobody else knows, believe it. I could tell you some things about Ray, too."

"All he said was that you were staying at the lake house for a while until you figured out what you wanted to do. That's all I know. It's all I want to know."

Kat paused.

"Oh."

We sat for a while and drank. I'd left my cell phone in the car, and I never wore a watch. The only mark of passing time was the movement of the sun in the sky and the growing number of crushed cans beside us. When the beers in the cooler ran out, I got us more. Behind us the party had continued. Paper plates and plastic cups littered the backyard, and Jimmy Buffett had been replaced by the Drive-By Truckers as the party got a little rowdier. Jackie Fulltone was playing darts by himself, casting covert glances over at the two girls who'd gone into the pool earlier. They were still topless, but now they were out of the water and sunning themselves. Their eyes were hidden behind their sunglasses, and judging by the laxness of their bodies, I was fairly sure they were asleep.

A large group had gathered at the outdoor TV, watching NC State play Georgia Tech. Tech was winning, but the game was close enough to keep everyone's attention. I saw Ray with Diego. They were talking to Rockwell Riggs. On the low, glass-topped table in front of them, I spied a small mountain of cocaine. Riggs was only halfway paying attention to the others. His head no longer looked like a grape about to pop, and he concentrated mostly on the blow in front of him, chopping it fine with a razor blade and then tasting a little from one finger.

I had an idea that Riggs wouldn't know cocaine from baby laxative, but drugs had never been my jam anyway. Diego saw me, nudged Ray, who looked over. He was drunk or high or both. His eyes were bloodshot and his nose was fairly glowing in the late afternoon sun. He grinned at me, shot me with a forefinger, and went back to his conversation. I loaded up the little cooler and went back to Kat. By now, Ray's boat had disappeared from sight. Five-hundred and twenty miles of lakeshore. Fifty miles of water surface. Good luck finding her, Ray.

I laughed, and Kat asked me what was so funny. When I told

her, she joined me. Kat leaned her head against me, and I put my arm around her briefly, patting her between her shoulder blades.

"You know, you're the only guy in the locker room who's never hit on me," she said. "Why is that?"

I tilted my head, shifted away so I could turn halfway toward her. "You were with Penny."

The air was turning colder. I could see gooseflesh rising on Kat's upper bare skin. She crossed her arms over her chest and shivered.

"Most of the boys don't care about that," she said. "They think that the only reason a woman's in a lesbian relationship is because she's never had the right dick."

I grunted. I was pretty sure that I had said and thought the same thing myself at one time, but it didn't seem prudent to bring it up at that moment.

"You are a terrible conversationalist, Alex Donovan." Kat's hand was on my leg. I didn't want to make any more of that than it might have meant. We'd both had a lot to drink.

"Hell of a listener, though."

Kat leaned in and kissed me on the cheek. She smelled like warm vanilla, like what I imagine heaven must smell like. We sat there and watched the sun go down over the trees in the west, letting the eerie springtime shadows play across the water. Behind us, the party raged on.

FIFTEEN

TWO HOURS BEFORE bell time, and everyone crowded into catering for the pre-production meeting. Writers handed out scripted promos and run sheets with times detailed down to fifteen-second increments. The way it worked, every writer was responsible for a different segment. In a three-hour TV show, that meant that there were a lot of writers. One by one, they broke down the show by segment.

By then everyone had changed into their gear. This meeting was old hat for most of the veterans in the locker room, and hardly any of them paid attention to the writers. They played on their phones, checking social media or playing games. A couple of them had earbuds in, listening to anything other than what management said. They were either established stars who could get away with things like that or talent so mired in the low card that they had zero chance of ever moving up toward the middle of the pack or main events. The younger boys and rookies were too excited—just plain happy to be on the big show—to fake being casual, and they paid attention to every word.

Digger was there, on the opposite side of the room, studiously not looking at me. Couldn't really blame him for that one, though. His face looked like it was put through a meat grinder, raw and red, with a large brace and bright white medical tape bracketing his nose. I didn't see his minions anywhere, but I wasn't sure that I'd even recognize them at this point. My concentration had been almost totally on Marcus Digger.

No matter how bad Digger looked, I was no prize, either. My palms were scraped raw, and my elbows and knees were missing hunge patches of skin. I had cuts on my face and head, and I felt like a walking bruise. I looked better than Digger, but not by much. I knew that I was going to hurt for the next week or two. But Digger wasn't going to be on TV that night, either. That was some small satisfaction.

I was too old to be fighting. All I wanted to do was go home and go to sleep. Instead, here I was, listening to the breakdown of a TV show I didn't watch anymore, and one that I certainly wasn't going to appear on. Scott Prichard had rounded up some sweat pants and a long-sleeved tee for me to replace the clothes that Digger ruined, and I leaned against the back wall of the room.

Mike Austin wormed his way through the crowded group of wrestlers until he was beside me. He put his lips near my ear. "Malone's fucking pissed. Did you have to fuck Digger up like that? We won't be able to use him on TV for weeks. The fans are going to wonder what happened."

"Tell them he got jumped by nine Marines in a bar outside Syracuse," I said.

Austin paused to peer over at Digger, who still wasn't looking this way.

"Jesus," he said. "That might fucking work."

My phone buzzed with an unfamiliar number, and I slipped out of the room to answer it. It was Aldeman, the cop who had taken my statement that morning. I went to the Gorilla position, where the monitors were dark for the moment. This was the only time that evening when the place would be quiet.

"Do you know where Mr. Wilder was staying? We can't find a record of him at any hotel in the metro area."

I thought about it for a second. "He told me that he drove over from Atlanta. He may not have gotten a hotel room."

"Then where was he going to sleep, Mr. Donovan?"

"I have no idea."

"Did he plan to crash with you?"

"He never mentioned it," I said. "And he would have said something if he'd wanted to stay."

There was silence on the other end of the phone as Aldeman thought things over. Something was pinging in the back of my own brain. I wasn't sure what it was yet, but I knew that it would come to me. I just needed my own time to think.

"He said he drove here from Atlanta."

"That's right."

"What kind of car did he drive?"

"I don't know," I said, "I never saw—wait, he told me. He rented a Toyota. We were laughing about it, because it was something he wouldn't have been caught dead driving back when we first knew each other."

Aldeman grunted in satisfaction.

"Where did he rent from?"

I switched the phone to my other hand.

"He didn't say, but probably from one of the airport kiosks."

"Right, right. Was there a key fob or anything that you saw, anything that would have had the rental company's name on it?"

I took my time answering, because I wanted Aldeman to know that I was thinking my answer through.

"I don't remember one," I said. "But if I think of it, I'll let you know."

I ended the call and went back to catering. The place looked like a tornado had hit while I was away. Barely a scrap of food left. I found some turkey breast, a couple of slices of cheese, and a hard roll, and put together a makeshift sandwich for myself. It was weird that the cops couldn't find a hotel reservation for Ray. Looking in the metro area had been a good idea in theory, but Ray would have wanted to stay in Birmingham. He would have wanted to be close to the nightlife in the city, not out in the suburbs.

When I thought about my time in wrestling, the time I had been around Ray Wilder almost every day, the one thing I knew was that Ray was a creature of habit. Even if he never went to his hotel room for anything more than a nap, he still had a reservation. Often it was in my name.

Nowadays he didn't have someone like me to run interference for him, and I still didn't know who he had gotten close to. Most of the old guard was gone, and the new faces in the locker room avoided hotel bars. If you weren't ready to drink like a fish and chase every piece of tail in the place, then you probably wouldn't hang around with Ray.

Jackie Fulltone was retired and out of the life. Dandy Sullivan died in an Omaha hotel room under an enthusiastic prostitute. Rockwell Riggs was doing time in a Pennsylvania prison for muling drugs. Scotty Prichard was a lackey, a hanger-on. Ray wouldn't have trusted Scotty because he was technically part of management, and one of the ways you stayed in management was that you told Malone Tomlinson everything. And no matter if they had buried the hatchet, Ray wouldn't trust Mike Austin with anything of consequence. Not after all of the time they'd spent hating each other backstage.

Austin could have set Digger on me, but I didn't think so. He and Scotty had helped even the odds in the alley behind the Boutwell. If Austin had been behind it, all he would have had to do is leave Digger and his buddies alone, and I wouldn't be anything more than a smear on the pavement by now.

I just wasn't sure what to do next. Maybe on a good day I could have pieced together what had actually happened to Ray, but my head was foggy from the beating I'd taken, and I just didn't seem to be able to ask the right questions. I was no kind of detective at all. Mostly I felt like an old boat, adrift on the water. I had no direction, and every time I tried to find one, another wave hit me and pushed me farther from my destination.

A roadie moved by me, clearly on a mission.

"Doors are open," he whispered as he went by. I found myself wandering to Gorilla again, with its monitors and sound boards. Now everything was lit up, as technicians made minor adjustments to achieve the rolling wall of sound that it seemed like every major production wanted. Maybe if the fans were worried about their ear drums rupturing, they wouldn't care about whether the show was good or bad.

Malone leaned in front of a pair of monitors, checking a headset that would allow him to talk directly into his commentators' ears. He produced every live show, feeding the announcers lines that he thought were important. I breezed past and went to the curtain, where several talents were peeking through to watch the fans stream in.

I knew how they felt. When I had been on the roster, I liked to look at the crowd before I went out. It gave me a jolt to watch the marks come through the doors and find their seats.

This crowd was relatively light, at least so far. I knew as the bell time neared that the arena would fill up. Birmingham people always thought they were a little too cool for wrestling, right up until they found themselves in line to buy a ticket. It'd been that way since the territory days, and now that the city considered itself something of a hub for the "new South," it was doubly true. There were a lot of things to do in Birmingham, great restaurants and bars, a lot of nightlife.

But when wrestling was at the Boutwell, people packed in. There is something about a Southern city that longs for its roots, and this is doubly true for a place like Birmingham, which is in many ways still a young city for the Deep South. It's the kind of place that isn't quite sure what its identity is, so you get the hipsters and the urban renewal artists. You get the yogurt shops and yoga studios, or places where you can get a bespoke haircut and hand-selected "vintage" clothing, all for a premium price. You get a Double-A baseball team with its roots in the Negro League. You get kids from all over the state who come to Birmingham because it's what the country folks think of as the big city.

So why are they so drawn to wrestling? People's lives are short, but their memories are long. They remember Bearcat Brown and Len Rossi at the Boutwell, the first interracial tag team in the Deep South. Rossi, always in great shape, was an unlikely hero who found his niche in eastern Tennessee and north and central Alabama. A kid from Utica, New York, he somehow connected deeply with the fans in Knoxville, Chattanooga, Huntsville, and Birmingham, and he was a reliable draw for promoters like John Cazana and Nick Gulas. Rossi and Bearcat faced down dastardly duos like the Fabulous Fargoes, Jackie and Don, in wild brawls that spilled blood and drew money all over the South.

The old-timers remember Sputnik Monroe, who regularly got arrested for being a white man who did his drinking in Blacks-only bars. Promoters would bail Sputnik out and then he would go on TV and cut promos about his experiences in the segregated areas of town, and invite "his people" to show up to the arena to watch him.

Dollars poured in, and everyone made money.

One of the kids at the curtain turned around. His short blonde hair was spiked in front like a shark's dorsal in, and the two-day growth of beard along his jaw was artfully maintained. The kid was in great shape, better than I ever was. His eyes lit up when he saw me, and he reached forward to clasp my hand.

"Mr. Donovan," he said. "I'm Mack Shelton. It's an honor. Big fan of your work."

I guess that's something that the kids can get away with saying these days, even though we would have been roasted for it back in my day. God, when did I get old? I thanked the kid and started to turn away. But then I thought better of it.

"Hey, can you tell me something?"

The kid fairly jumped at the chance, like a puppy eager for a treat.

"Yes, sir, whatever I can."

"Who did Ray Wilder hang out with backstage?"

Shelton looked confused for a moment. He used his palms to check the big spike in his hair, then chuckled to himself.

"He, uh, well, you know—it's different now. We don't really hang out a lot like you guys did, you know? A lot of us are in our own little world most of the time."

"Did you see him much?"

Shelton shook his head so hard that I thought it might come loose from his thick neck.

"He really kept to himself a lot. I've only been here a couple of years, you know? He wasn't really what I'd call social."

That didn't sound like Ray at all. When he wasn't looking for a party, Ray was the party. What the hell was going on with him before he died? I thanked the kid and went to find Mike Austin.

I found Austin in a narrow hallway working on promo lines with a Black man who looked like he could bench press a Buick in each hand. I stood a short distance away so as not to interrupt them until they were done. Austin wasn't so much giving the wrestler promo lines as much as giving him advice about how to put the writers' words into his own voice.

"I know they got a script but nobody gives a good goddamn about the script," Austin said. "Here's what you gotta get across."

He told the guy the thrust of the story, and the wrestler nodded along. I didn't pay attention to the details, because it was none of my concern. When they were done, Mike looked up and saw it was me.

"Oh, hey, Alex. Meet Porter 'the House' Dunn." We shook, and Porter enveloped my fingers in his hand. He gave me the veteran handshake, with no pressure at all. I was glad. He could have crushed my knuckles into dust if he had wanted to.

"Pleasure," Dunn said, flashing even white teeth in the dim light of the hallway. He was an easy six-seven, and carried three hundred pounds on his frame. None of it was fat; he looked like a perfect physical specimen. As I stood there next to him, I felt like a manual typewriter next to a modern tablet computer. He was bigger, faster, and stronger than I would ever be. He could probably do all the flippy stuff that all of the current roster was expected to do. I would have never made it in the modern wrestling world. My teeth weren't perfect, my hairline fled early, and no matter how much I worked out and ate right, I couldn't have produced a single abdominal muscle. But I looked—and sounded—like I could kick someone's ass, and that's what I had always relied on.

"Any idea who was Ray hanging around with, toward the end?"

Austin thought about it. Out of the corner of my eye, I saw Porter Dunn look away from me. Maybe it was nothing. Maybe it was something. I wasn't sure.

"I don't know," Austin said. "You have to realize that things are different now. I got a lot of responsibilities backstage. Ray and I had settled our business, but we weren't ever going to be close."

I looked at Dunn. His eyes went everywhere but to me.

"Mike, what aren't you telling me? Goddammit, I'm blind here. Fucking smarten me up, man."

Porter put a hand on my shoulder. He didn't want to lift his eyes to meet mine. But when he did, I could tell that they were full of sincerity. And pity.

"Mike don't want to say it," he said. "But Ray didn't have a whole lot of friends anymore. His rep was that he'd fuck you over if you let your guard down around him. They don't want us to close the door and take care of that ourselves anymore, so we left him alone. About the only people he talked to was Malone and Austin here, sometimes Scotty."

I hated the picture I had in my mind of Ray Wilder increasingly isolated, friendless in a locker room full of people who were constantly worried about their own spot on the roster. The wrestling business can breed paranoia if you're not careful. And a guy like Ray, for him to just be ignored in the locker room, that had to feed into his own anxieties.

Next to me, Austin was looking at his shoes. I understood that feeling. I'd learned things about Ray that day that I didn't want to face, either. At the end, my so-called best friend had been isolated and pushed away by the locker room, and the boys were the only family Ray had ever known.

For years, wrestling was a home for the misfits, the outlaws, the people who couldn't find a life anywhere else. If you weren't physically deformed—and sometimes if you were—you could find a place in wrestling. It was a home for giants and little people, for nature boys and oddities, for deviants, for outcasts, for wild children never forced to grow up, and for the friends and family who protected and enabled them. We were an island of misfit toys, and maybe I had only been fooling myself that I had ever left.

That was the problem right there. Had I ever been a friend Ray? Or had I just been the longest-running in a series of enablers? I'd driven him to shows when he was drunk off his ass or so goddamn high that he could have doubled for a kite. I'd stood back-to-back with him and fought off drums and rioters and crazy assholes; I'd been with him when he had issues with management. I'd seen him at his best, and at his worst. And I'd never flinched.

SIXTEEN

March 18, 2001
The Washington-Jefferson Hotel
New York City

NEARLY THREE MONTHS into the new year, and the wrestling business changed for good. Malone Tomlinson purchased ICW, and Ray and I were two weeks into our new contracts. Malone had chosen to honor ICW's deals with us because we were two of the only viable properties left in the company after Bill Cunningham sold out to a media company who was more interested in selling cheap advertising than putting on a wrestling show. Bill was off somewhere counting his money, and Malone now had what he'd always wanted: total control of the wrestling world.

Sure, we could have signed big-money deals in Japan. But even though the schedule would have been favorable in a couple of respects: fewer matches, more time off, there would have been even more hassles. International travel. Longer, more physically intense matches. Days spent riding tour buses with the boys instead of flying first-class to the town and being driven to the arena in a stretch limo. The food would be different, too, and although the language barrier wouldn't matter a whole hell of a lot in the ring—in the mid-20th century, Terry and Dory Funk had ensured that English would be the language of pro wrestling in Japan—we would need an interpreter nearly all the time in the real world.

So we had signed with Malone. It was Ray's second time around with New York-based UCW. In the early 1990s, Ray and Bill Cunningham fell out. Bill wasn't getting any younger, and he'd brought in a layer of management to separate himself from the day-to-day business of the locker room. The new management hadn't been fond of Ray, had in fact made a severe miscalculation about his popularity both in the locker room and in ticket sales. They sidelined both Ray and me for weeks at a time, put the world title on a young surfer dude named Mustang, and expected things to take off.

Wrestling fans need good guys and bad guys, babyfaces and heels. The business works best by using archetypes that operate in a black-and-white world, with little gray area. While that has changed somewhat over the years, in the early 1990s, Ray and I were the best heels in the business, and Mustang needed us. There has to be an antagonist for the hero. Only the new management didn't realize that. They were much more interested in merchandising Mustang as the face of the company.

When ticket sales to live events and TV ratings crashed, they didn't understand what happened. But it got Ray and me back on TV, and Mustang dropped the world title back. In truth, I think the kid was happy to do it. It's difficult to carry a whole company on your shoulders. Ratings and ticket sales increased. But when it came time to renegotiate Ray's deal, the new management balked again. Imagine telling your biggest star to go fuck himself. That's essentially what Bill Cunningham's new management did to Ray. The Wild Child took the ICW title belt to New York and proclaimed himself the undisputed world champion. That angle made big money for UCW and Ray, while I was taken off TV for nearly a year. Ray eventually came back South, as I knew he would. But by then Malone Tomlinson's UCW was clearly the big league, and the rest of us were just pretending otherwise.

"You'll like Malone," Ray said. He was lying on the big bed in the Washington-Jefferson Hotel on W. 51st Street, while I sat in an armchair made for a much smaller person. My feet rested on the corner of the bed. The rooms were tiny, but clean, and we'd each taken adjoining rooms to make them feel like suites. My rooms were on the fourth floor, Ray's on the sixth. They were identical. Lilliputian bathrooms, huge beds with thick white comforters and clean white sheets. Nothing much in the way of anything extra at all.

The hotel called itself a 'boutique' hotel, meaning no one bothered with amenities like room service or a hotel bar. It was pleasant, as it always was, to hang out and shoot the shit with Ray, but I was getting hungry, and that probably made me worse company than usual.

"He always run late?" I asked, mostly just to be saying something.

"He's not like Bill, trying to run a national business out of a converted gas station. Malone's got the real deal going up here. Give him some time. I'm telling you, he's first-class all the way."

"All right," I said. "I'll love the guy. Maybe I'll marry his sister."

Ray snorted.

"She's out of your league."

"Too bad your mom wasn't."

Ray threw a pillow at me. I caught it before it could hit me, fluffed it a little, and tucked it between my lower back and the undersized armchair. Neither of us was drinking yet. I wanted to make a good impression on the new boss, I guess. Ray was the kind of guy where you could never tell. He drank every day that I knew him, but he never seemed to want it. I drank some days, and didn't drink sometimes. I was afraid that if I wanted it too much that the alcohol would have a hold on me and not the other way around.

A TV bolted into an upper corner of the room showed the local weather. The snow that still existed on the Manhattan streets looked sooty and gray, the way the rest of the city felt to me. Eventually someone knocked on the door. Ray swung his feet to the floor, but I was closer. I opened it, and there was Malone Tomlinson.

He was bigger than he looked on television, maybe my height. Black hair swept back from an unlined forehead, with a deeply dimpled chin. His face was tanned, and his teeth were white and even. The Glen plaid suit he wore was obviously tailored, cinched at the waist to emphasize his broad shoulders and narrow waist. He didn't wear a tie with his suit, and that made me like him more than I thought I would. In those first few moments, Malone Tomlinson came off as a likeable, we're-all-just-folks kind of guy.

"Alex Donovan, I recognize you," he said. "You're a hell of a hand." He extended a large, hard-knuckled hand. He held a heavy leather briefcase in the other hand, clutching it close to his body without seeming to. We shook. His palm was heavily calloused despite a gleaming manicure. "I bet you boys are hungry. How do you feel about Mexican?"

"Love it," I said, and a couple of minutes later we were dressed in coats and hats, on the street, heading toward 9th Ave. We went down the sidewalk with Malone shifting his grip on the briefcase every few minutes.

Malone led us to a hole-in-the-wall Mexican place called Mi Nidito. At first glance, the place was unimpressive. The tables were low and featured mismatched chairs. A postage-stamp of a bar loomed in the back next to the kitchen pass-through. We snagged a table and the waiter brought us menus. I was sitting there thinking that if Ray thought this kind of place was first-class, he must have taken one hell of a char shot to the head recently. But the multi-colored corn chips our server brought to the table were obviously fresh-made, and the salsa served with it was thick, slightly sweet, and spicy.

I started to open a menu, and Malone told me not to bother.

"A place like this is authentic," he said. "The menu's for the tourists."

He spoke to the waiter in a burst of Spanish so fast that I had no way of following it even if I'd spoken more than a few words of the language. I'd studied Spanish in high school, although 'studied' might be a little strong. The only really useful phrase I remembered was 'Donde esta el bano?' … which came in handy more often than one might think. The waiter grinned, answered something just as hard to follow, and went away.

"I took the liberty of ordering margaritas for us," Malone said. "I hope that's all right with you."

A few minutes later, our waiter came through the crowded restaurant, a circular serving tray held aloft and balanced in one hand. When he reached our table, he brought the tray down and unloaded three of the largest margaritas I'd ever seen. The glasses were literally the size of fishbowls, with ice cubes like nordic floes swimming in the liquid. The rim of each glass was thickly clotted with enough coarse salt that it looked like fresh snowfall. If the margaritas had been large, that would have been one thing. But they were also the best cocktail I'd ever had. As I drank some of my drink, my regard for Malone Tomlinson grew.

"Ray, the fans are going to be familiar with you," he said, "so I thought we could start off with you and Alex in a tag team, kind of build him until our audience gets to know him. Let's put the tag belts on you right out of the gate."

Ray had already drunk half of his margarita, and I wasn't far behind.

"That's fine," Ray said, "but everyone is going to know Alex already. The last time I worked for you, everyone wanted to know why I left him behind in the other promotion."

I'd wondered that same thing myself, but it didn't seem like the best time to bring that up. Instead, I concentrated on my drink.

"Is that right," Malone said.

"Absolutely. People are going to be hot for us. They're gonna go out of their minds."

"Is there a team that we've got under contract that you'd like to work?"

At that moment, Tom and Tim Brecher, two brothers who had each won All-American honors at the University of Iowa, were the world tag team champs. They had made the transition that a lot of amateurs can't, from shoot wrestling to working. It was always always a challenge working those kinds of guys, and I knew that Ray wouldn't want to do it for long. Guys with amateur-style credentials sometimes balk at putting over anyone they don't consider "real" wrestlers. They haven't fully "gotten" the business yet. The difference between a good pro wrestler and a good amateur is that the only metric for a good pro is that he puts asses in seats.

By that metric, Ray and I were miles better than the Brechers.

"You got a team out of Mexico, right?"

"Naturally," Malone said. "Picador del Norte and the Toreador. They're mid-card right now, but I don't see any reason we can't move them up. They're a good team."

"The way we sell, we'll make them a great team," Ray said. He elbowed me in the side, and I grinned. Malone took a small sip of his drink and studied me, a wrinkle between his perfectly groomed eyebrows.

"You don't say much, do you?"

I thought about just shaking my head, but realized that I would be doing it only for my amusement.

"I let Ray do the talking," I said. "I do the work. Things usually work out better for me that way."

"I like a man who knows his strengths."

Just then the waiter came back with huge platters of carnitas, tortillas, rice, beans, and an assortment of other dishes. I was hungry enough that I dove into the food and didn't look up from my plate until I'd put away several tortillas stuffed with pork, cheese, and beans. I asked the waiter for a glass of water, and then listened as Ray and Malone talked business.

"You know Tom and Tim aren't going to like being pushed out of the title picture," Malone said. "They may get a little testy with you."

Ray chewed thoughtfully and swallowed before he answered.

"I've known them a long time," he said. "It won't be a problem."

Malone rubbed his fingertips carefully across his cheeks, a gesture I would come to know well in the future. He didn't have his electric shaver in his hand, but he unconsciously moved his hands to mimic the movement, and I recall thinking of it as a way that he soothed himself. We spent a long time at the restaurant, and I found out that Ray was right—Malone Tomlinson was a guy who wanted to do things in a first-class way. One of the ways he did that was making sure that a country boy like me went to a neighborhood restaurant instead of a Michelin-starred gastro pub that served hummingbird tongue and baby's-breath as the main course.

We talked over the best way to get the belts off of the Brechers, finding a few options to make it happen without hurting anyone's ego. By the time lunch was over, we'd reached a handshake deal to get the belts by the first of May, and if all went as we thought it would, we'd keep them for nearly a year.

Malone paid the tab, and we left. He went toward Times Square, while Ray and I headed back to the hotel. Ray had Tomlinson's briefcase in his hand, swinging it along jauntily as walked, just as if it belonged to him. I pretended not to notice, and Ray wasn't going to bring it up. When we got back to the hotel, we took the elevator up. I got out on my floor, and Ray continued to his.

I cracked the seal on a fresh bottle once I opened my door.

SEVENTEEN

FINDING MALONE'S CAR was easy. It was the only Rolls Royce—in fact, the only car—on the basement floor of the parking garage. Above us, at ground level, the marks were driving in and paying their ten bucks or whatever the hell it was for the privilege of parking next to the Boutwell. Down here, Malone had everything to himself. His driver leaned against the door, his eyes glued to his smartphone. Wireless earbuds plugged his ears. Child's play to sneak up on the deaf and blind. By the time the driver realized I was there, it was far too late. I doubled my arm, driving with my forearm and connecting hard along his jaw, the blow sounding like the butt of an axe striking a watermelon.

The driver went down, his head cracking against the Rolls' side panel, leaving a dent in the mirrored silver finish. His smartphone shattered against the concrete.

Oops.

I fished through the guy's pockets until I found the keys to the car. Beep the trunk open, then stuff the driver in. It sounds easy when I say it like that, but it wasn't. Not really. An unconscious human body is an unwieldy thing, arms and legs loose and

121

flopping like an uncoordinated newborn. I dragged the driver behind the car, and after a few moments, he tried to stand. He couldn't quite make it. He caught his hands on the open trunk lid, pulled himself up. I slammed the trunk on his fingers, and he screamed. The sound echoed against the concrete around us, a sound louder than the clap of creation.

But that's part of the problem with the kind of privacy Malone bought. When you need help, no one can hear you beg for it.

The trunk yawned open again, and this time I was able to get the driver's hip higher than the opening. Tears ran from his eyes, and he clutched his injured hands to his chest. Soft chuffs of breath came in hot bursts as he tried to say something. I kept him pinned against the trunk while I yanked the emergency pull-handle from the trunk.

"Please," he finally moaned. "Please. Don't. Don't —"

He folded into the space, and I slammed the lid on him. Around me, this level of the garage was empty. There were security cameras everywhere, probably a recording of what I'd just done. But no one came to check. Next door, the show was about to start. Fans would be pouring through the gates, the Boutwell staff would be scanning tickets, and security would have their hands full with fans who wanted to get a little too rowdy.

Malone always produced the first hour of live TV for UCW. He'd get a read on the crowd reactions, communicate specific lines of verbiage he wanted his announcers to use, keep time, and often re-write later segments of the show if he didn't like the crowd reaction. However, once the tone of the show was set during that first hour, Malone would usually hand off the producing duties to someone else. In the old days, that wouldn't have happened. But Malone had been fifty—or near it—by the time he triumphed over every other bit of competition in the wrestling world. Now he was seventy years old or just past it, and he couldn't keep up the same schedule that he'd once enjoyed.

At 8:01 p.m., I cranked the Rolls and turned on the headlights.

In the trunk, the driver was thrashing around, rocking the big car. I slammed my palm against the trunk and told him to be still.

"It won't be long," I said. "You'll be fine. This will all be over soon."

One way or another was the part I didn't say out loud. And then I stood behind a concrete support to wait for Malone.

He came, as he always did, with purpose. Malone Tomlinson didn't wait around for a whole lot of anything. He strode across the bare and stained concrete floor, his eyes fixed on the gray ghost of the car that would whisk him away to his hotel room. Where he'd probably work some more before bed.

If you'd never seen him before, you'd swear Malone Tomlinson was decades younger than he actually was. He didn't walk like an old man. There was still spring in his step. But from the moment he banged open the door to the parking garage, he hadn't looked at anything besides the Rolls. When he reached for the car door was when I stepped out from my hiding place. It was a long step from me to Tomlinson, and in that space I gathered every little bit of momentum I could and hit him with a hard right fist in the kidney.

Malone gasped, a sick, wet gagging sound. He stumbled forward against the car, dropped his briefcase, and tried to get his balance back. I kicked his ankles apart so that he had to lean against the Rolls to maintain his balance. Then I really went to work. Kidney punches, short and hard, ripped from the hips. Every last one of them found a home. Malone tried to get away, tried to turn and face me. Every time he did, I got a fist full of hair and banged his head on the roof of the Rolls.

Eventually he stopped trying, and I ran out of steam. Grabbing Malone by the jacket, I spun him around and slapped him across the face, forehand and backhand.

"We've been fucking around with this for too long," I said, and my voice with thick,clotted with violence and rage. "Who killed Ray?"

"I'll have you killed," Malone whispered. He couldn't straighten up. In the gleam of the overhead fluorescents, Malone's pink scalp was visible through his thinning, gray hair. His face was slack with visible wrinkles like a topographical map of age. Saliva ran from one corner of his mouth, and he fell forward to his knees and puked on the floor. I was just quick enough that I didn't get splashed with it.

Shame tried to rise in my heart, and I pushed it down, tried to let the rage carry me forward. But I couldn't help thinking about it as I stood over my old boss. I'd beaten up a senior citizen. The Malone who was the target of all my anger was twenty years in the past and unreachable now.

No. Fuck that. I needed to find out who killed Ray. I lowered my chin to my chest, moved around the puddle of vomit, and grabbed Malone. He scrambled for his briefcase, but I kicked it away from him.

"It's just you and me now," I said, and forced myself to laugh. "You know how many promoters have wanted a moment like this? You ran everybody else out of the business, Malone. You're the king now, the only one left, and no one is coming to your rescue."

Malone didn't say anything, just scrabbled away from me like a crab trying to escape a net. His Rolex scraped along the floor, the sound like metallic fingernails against a chalkboard.

"You gonna have me killed? Like Ray?"

Malone held a hand up between us. A surrender. A prayer.

"I didn't kill Ray," he said. "You have my word."

"Yeah, you did." I came closer. Now Malone was on one skinny hip, one heel almost beneath him. I felt like a wolf watching its weak prey. Waiting for the right moment.

It didn't take long. Malone came off the ground with a rush, and if he were a younger man, it would have worked. As he rose, he reached behind his back and came up with a black rectangle in one hand. Electricity crackled between a pair of metal studs as he swung for me.

The thing about stun guns is that they're usually not lethal. When I saw Malone come up with the damn thing, I knew that I was going to get popped. Just like a knife fight. Someone comes at you with a blade, you know you're gonna get cut. Maybe it would have turned out differently if I hadn't already put a beating on him, but the kidney punches had slowed him down. I sidestepped and threw a left hand that caught Malone in the side of the neck just before I felt the bite from the miniature lightning rod.

I never went out, not completely. The world grayed around me, and the fringes of my consciousness became ragged and worn like the edges of an old blanket.

I sat up. My body trembled, and my pants were wet where my bladder had let go. It didn't hurt, exactly, but the experience of being separated from my ability to control my body was one of the more unpleasant sensations I'd ever endured. Beside me, Malone was still down. His breath came in ragged gasps. I crawled to him on my hands and knees, reached down and slapped his cheeks lightly. The overflowing red rage was gone. I felt empty, as though the jolt of electricity had re-set something in my soul.

Maybe it had. I put my ear to Malone's chest. His heartbeat was strong and even. My hands shook when I held them in front of my face, but the more the world swam back into focus, the more control I began to exert over my fine motor functions. I patted Malone's face until he groaned and rolled over. I was happy for him. Happy he wasn't dead. Happy I hadn't killed him. At some point it occurred to me that he might try to stun me again, and this time the effects might be a great deal worse.

I climbed to my feet, a herculean effort that left my head feeling like a balloon disconnected from my body. Next to the car, Malone was almost to his feet. He was using the Rolls' front tire and hood to give himself purchase. I wish I'd thought of that. Between us was the black flat rectangle, the little personal lightning bolt Malone had zapped me with. I saw it before he did and kicked it away. It went skittering across the floor like a wild animal looking for a place to hide.

Malone clawed for the door handle, trying to get into the car, get to something resembling safety. He wasn't quick enough. I took him by the collar and turned him around. His old, gray face was full of fear, and I felt a little spurt of triumph. Knuckles hard and white, I gripped his Oxford-weave shirt in my hands and pressed my forehead against his.

"Ray muled for you," I said. It wasn't a question, so Malone didn't answer.

"He was washed up, everybody on the roster hated him. You kept him around. For what?"

Malone hesitated.

"You're wearing a wire, aren't you?"

"I've always been straight with you, Malone." I shook him a little, and he cried out softly, like a baby having a bad dream.

"Don't," he said. "Don't."

"Ray muled for you."

"Y-yes. All right? Yes."

"What was he carrying?"

"Steroids, human growth hormone," Malone said quietly. "He was the pharmacy."

A light bulb went on somewhere in my head, and everything began to make sense. God damn it. Almost every wrestler—especially those of us who had come along in the 1980s—had used steroids at one time or another. They weren't illegal at that time, and it looked like a great deal. You got bigger, faster, and stronger. You could work out harder in the gym. You could go harder in the ring. Whatever anyone says, wrestling has always been a cosmetic business. Just like actors get their teeth bonded and bleached, or botox to ward off any incipient wrinkles, most wrestlers of my era have had a needle full of juice in the ass at some point.

Use was so open that sometimes wrestlers referenced their use in promos. Hercules Gonzalez once flexed at the camera while his manager pointed out Hercules' enormous physique. "You see this man? This man is the product of ten Dianabol a day, baby!"

When steroids had become illegal, they didn't go away. They went underground. Human growth hormone seemed like a safer—to say nothing of legal—alternative, too. Eventually, even though most of the locker room was on some kind of 'performance enhancer,' only a few guys would actually carry the stuff, which allowed promoters and talent to deny using. They were never caught with drugs. Then if you needed something, you went to the pharmacy.

Ray was a perfect mule. He was old now, not quite as old as Malone. He didn't have to keep up the same physique he'd had while he was in the ring, so he'd gotten off the juice.

But if Ray was acting as the pharmacy for Malone's locker room, what happened? Had something gone wrong?

"Did Ray want more money? Is that it? Was it too much?"

Malone shook his head, his eyes wide with fear.

"No—no," he said, voice trembling. "I got along with Ray, we worked it out. I swear to you, Donovan. I didn't have anything to do with Ray's death. He still had a suitcase full of stubb for me, and I don't even know where that is."

I believed him. He was so shaken by then that he would have told me anything that I wanted to know. And if Ray's pharmaceutical suitcase was missing, too, that meant that the killer knew what he did for Malone.

Son of a bitch. One of the boys really had killed him.

EIGHTEEN

January 4, 1994
Vienna, Austria

DON'T ASK ME how he did it, but Bill Cunningham managed to book a two-week tour of Europe for his ICW promotion. We wrestled in Dublin, London, Glasgow, Paris, Berlin, Stuttgart, Madrid, and points in-between. You would think I'd have lovely things to say about the sights, that I could describe to you everything that I saw and heard and felt. But the truth is that our schedule was so concentrated that what I experienced was a generally interchangeable series of airports and train rides and anonymous hotel rooms. Everything blended together, and jet lag had given me a headache that I tried to cure with local wines. Sometimes that helped, but most of the time I simply felt a little muzzy, as if a curtain had come down and smothered some small but vital part of my brain.

It didn't help that most of the crowds didn't know what to make of our traveling road show, but they at least seemed to enjoy the athleticism and the hard-hitting action that we brought to the shows.

A lot of wrestling has its base in pantomime, so that it can transcend language barriers. Fans should be able to tell good guys from bad guys just by their body language. You telegraph what you're going to do before you do it, and the movements are big, elaborate exaggerations so that people sitting in the nosebleed seats can still tell what's happening in the ring. That over-the-top expressiveness is toned down for TV, but you can still see it at house shows, the things they refer to now as 'live events.'

The bar that night was across the street from the hotel, and mostly it was a quiet night. Ray and I were there with Brian Middleton, a retired Welsh wrestler with a reputation for toughness that had been born in Billy Riley's 'Snake Pit' in Wigan, in the Lancashire region of England. Riley had drilled the boys in Wigan as if he were their personal devil. If professional wrestling was real, Middleton would have been a world champion many times over, despite his short stature. He was known as a 'hooker'—a wrestler who knows ways to cripple an opponent. Not just beat him.

Brain was part of a group of wrestlers like Karl Gotch, Ben Assirati, Tony Charles, Les Thornton, and Billy Robinson. Everything they did in the ring looked completely legitimate, and anyone who had been in the ring with them could attest that every move they utilized hurt like hell.

Middleton made his way from Britain's World of Sport wrestling, where he was a multi-time British Empire champion, to the US, where he was primarily featured as a perennial opponent to legendary world junior heavyweight champion, Danny Hodge. Hodge was likely the greatest amateur wrestler the United States had ever produced, with legendary ability both on the mat and with his fists. He and Middleton meshed perfectly in the ring, with Middleton's rough Wigan-style grappling perceived as a legitimate threat to Hodge's world title.

Brian Middleton made his American money, then he came back to Lancashire, where he retired and began teaching wrestling to new generations. He joined our European tour because he was so well known over there. Even though he wasn't wrestling anymore, he'd come out every night, sign some autographs, and referee the main event. That night at the bar, we'd gone through several pints, listening to Brian's stories told in his thick Welsh accent. Normally, Ray would be the one holding forth, but he had known Brian a long time and held him in such high regard that he was like me, sitting there mute and marveling at the tales the little Welshman could tell.

Brian never bought a drink for himself any night on the tour. Ray and I made sure of that.

Things were winding down that night, and some of the boys had gravitated over to our table. One of them was Psycho Stan Laurie, a perfectly sculpted physical specimen, an easy six-ten and three hundred pounds. He was headlining the cards most nights against Ray, and fans were really responding to him. He was a striking man, with cobalt blue eyes that did look psycho when he stared unblinking at you across the ring.

Psycho Stan was all show, though. Everyone knew that he was big and strong and fast, but he couldn't wrestle his way out of a wet paper bag. He also had a habit of getting injured in the late spring every year. During his supposed recovery, he'd take a few months off and go play semi-professional softball in his native Arkansas. Ray didn't like Stan because he thought Stan was unreliable, and Stan didn't like Ray because he thought that the hot crowds were just there to see him, and he felt he deserved the world title.

I don't know if Psycho Stan wanted to start something when he came over, or if he just kind of gravitated over and things developed after that.

"—so anyway, Hodge says to me that he's going home that night with a hammerlock, an' I told him that he'd never get it on me. No way. We went back an' forth a bit in the locker room, just teasing the hell out of each other. You know how he was. We go out there, and Hodge loved to just wrestle. He loved it when someone could go with 'im, so that's what I'd do. Everything but the finish was a real shoot. We'd get on the mat and it was like two snakes fucking, bound up so tight you couldn't tell who was who. All of a sudden, Hodge has my arm, got two hands on it, an' you know what Dan's grip is like—"

We all did. Danny Hodge could break pliers apart with the power in his hands. We'd all seen him crush apples into nothing more than juice and pulp. He claimed to have been born with double tendons in his hands, and for all I knew it could be true.

Hodge had been forced into retirement by a car accident. An almost unbeatable wrestler—unless he let you—Hodge had fallen victim to one of the very real dangers of professional wrestling. He'd fallen asleep at the wheel of his VW station wagon and driven off a Louisiana bridge and into a nine-feet deep creek. With water pouring into the car from all sides and in excruciating pain, Hodge clamped his hands around his own neck to stabilize himself and swam to shore by kicking his legs. He made it up the embankment, holding his neck all the while. A passing trucker radioed for help when he saw Hodge on the side of the road, and emergency surgery was needed to save Hodge's life. A trauma surgeon fused part of Hodge's hip to his spinal column to repair his broken neck. Danny Hodge had literally held his broken neck together by the force of his own grip.

He was lucky to make it out alive. A lot of wrestlers of that era didn't. Moondog Lonnie Mayne had been killed up in Oregon when he fell asleep at the wheel. Whitey Caldwell, a legend in the mountains of east Tennessee and the Kenucky hills, died in a car accident on his way home from a card in Morristown, Tennessee one night.

"—so he's pulling for the hammerlock, and I'm bloody screaming and laughing. I catch Danny's eye and he's grinnin' because he knows he's got one over on me. So I let go with me legs and just slither around. He's got my arm, but my body's free. I roll into the turn, he's on his back, just for a second. Not even long enough for the ref to get down there, but if we were going amateur rules, that's a pin. I hold him long enough so that he knows it, and then we're both back up, going again. He was going after me the whole time. Worst thing I ever did was escape that hammerlock. He made me pay for it every time after that."

Psycho Stan listened the whole time, drinking dark beer and wiping foam away from his mustache. His tightly permed hair fell to a long fringe in the back, and a bad dye job had turned it a particularly awful shade of orange, like a rotting midwest moon. His shoulders stretched the thin material of his t-shirt, which was nearly see-through. Look at him from behind, and you could see the minefield of acne that sprouted from his trapezius to nearly the middle of his back. He could not have looked more like a poster boy for steroids if he tried, but no one ever found them on him.

That was the year we were using KC Dillan, a referee and noted office stooge, as our pharmacy. KC was rail thin and no more than five-ten, a religious zealot when he wasn't working the shows. Sometimes he roomed with Stan, who was currently incensed that anyone had dared to suggest that he could hang with Danny Hodge on the mat.

"You pinned Hodge?" Stan asked. "I don't believe that."

I rubbed a hand across my face and peeked over at Ray, who covered his grin with a hand. Maybe Stan had a right to his opinion. He'd grown up in Arkansas, had seen Hodge wrestle … and in fact it was rumored that Hodge had made a call to Bill Watts, who promoted the Mid-South territory, to get him to take a look at Stan. But Brian Middleton was a real-deal wrestler, and Psycho Stan should have known that.

"I'll take your opinion into consideration, young man, while I'm takin' a piss. I'll weigh it against me cock, an' whichever matters less is the one I'll toss away, see?"

Stan scratched absently at his throat where he'd missed a spot shaving that morning.

"You talk big for a man who don't even reach my kneepads."

Brian set his empty pint glass down hard on the table. But his eyes were full of merriment, and I detected a smile playing along his lips. Brian Middleton was long retired, but he had been wrestling all of his life. He was looking forward to whatever came.

"You know when I was in the business, the only boys who used knee pads were the ones who had to give the promoter a blowjob to even get on the card."

It took a moment for the insult to sink into Psycho Stan's brain, but when it finally did, he erupted. Stan backhanded Middleton out of his seat, but the little Welshman bounced up like a rubber ball, waist-locking the larger man before he could stand completely upright. Brain used his lower center of gravity as a pivot, driving Stan to his knees. At that point, they were almost the same height.

Stan tried to rise, but by the time he knew that he was in trouble, the fight had already been decided. Brian scissored his legs around Stan's torso while he slithered his left arm underneath Stan's chin. He locked his left hand into the crook of his right elbow and folded his right hand behind Stan's head. Brian began to squeeze, and Psycho Stan's face turned a deep shade of purple.

Within a few seconds, Stan went completely limp. His arms splayed at his sides, and his legs were completely lifeless. Brian released the hold and said, "Will somebody get the ox offa me? He's heavy as hell."

Ray and I each grabbed a boat-sized foot, and we dragged Stan away. Brian stood up, used his palms to brush the front of his slacks clean of any lint or dust, and sat down at the table as though nothing had happened. It took everything Ray and I could do to roll Stan onto his side so that if he puked, he wouldn't swallow it and die. Then we rejoined Brian.

"Your main-event boy, eh?" Brian asked, his voice dry. "Well, I suppose they don't make them like they used to. If he was as tough as he looks, I guess we'd all be in trouble, wouldn't we?"

He was in the middle of telling us a story about working against Archie Gouldie, who had barnstormed the southeastern US as the Mongolian Stomper when the bartender arrived with a couple of burly Viennese cops, who wanted to know what the hell was going on. At this point, Stan was sitting up, rubbing his temples like he had the worst hangover in the world. And he may have.

After a tense couple of minutes—and a thick wad of bills passed quietly between Brian and the bartender—we took the party back to the hotel. Stan went to his room, and we went to Brian's.

We made the switch from beer to Glen Slitsia, a wheat-based German whisky, when we got up to the room. I'd never had it, though Ray and Brian both assured me that it was good. We drank and told stories until nearly three a.m., when Brian answered a knock at the door.

Psycho Stan boiled into the room. In one hand he held a pair of needle-shaped scissors, small ones like most of us carried in our bags. They were useful for lots of things, including snipping off sutures if you ever had to sew a cut closed. Stan stabbed Brian once, and then again. Ray saw what was happening and started moving toward the door. So did I, but by that time I was so drunk that the bed got in the way and I tripped over it. Stan must've gotten Brian with the scissors seven or eight times by then. The floor was slick with blood. Ray and I didn't even try to help Brian. We went for Stan instead, trying to pin his arms to his sides.

Stan wasn't having any of it, though. He was enormously strong, and he was planning to kill Brian for embarrassing him in the bar. At that point, he was so angry that he didn't care who he hurt. He really had lived up to his nickname. He slashed my side with the sharp blades, and I felt them rattle against my ribs. Soon, my own blood was pattering against the floor, joining the rest of the mess.

Even if Ray and I weren't successful at subduing Stan, we distracted him long enough for Brian to get hold of his hand. In most wrestling, small-joint locks—holds that depend upon using leverage and torque on fingers or wrists—are frowned upon. But Brian was an encyclopedia of wrestling, and he was in a life-or-death situation. If someone didn't get Stan under control, he was going to kill everyone in the room.

Brian trapped Stan's hand with both of his own, using his already bleeding body to isolate the limb even further. With one quick twist, he dislocated Stan's thumb and index finger. The scissors clattered to the floor as the huge man howled in range and tried to shake Ray and me off, but we held on.

Brian plucked the scissors from where they landed and went to work. The first time the blades bit into Stan, he screamed like a frightened child and tried to back away. He made it into the hallway, but Brian followed. He stabbed Stan in the neck and abdomen several times, and then he got mean. He punched the thin, narrow scissor blades between two of Stan's ribs and punctured his lung.

Stan had held on until he hit the far side of the hallway, then he crumpled. First his knees gave way. Then the rest of his body. When he fell, Brian stopped coming forward. His hands were bathed in crimson, and small flecks of blood—at that point, I wasn't sure if they were his, or Stan's, or mine—dotted his face. Around us, other hotel guests had begun to stick their heads out of their doors to see what was going on. Blood soaked the floor. Stan's eyes were blank and far away, even though I could still see his chest rise and fall, shallow movements that began to slow. He was going to need help, and a lot of it, if he was going to live.

"I think I need to sit down, mate," Brian said just before he sort of swooned down to the floor. Now that the fight was over, I didn't feel so good, either. A long flap of skin hung loose along my left side. I sat down next to Brian and we waited for help to arrive.

Ray was unhurt. When the paramedics came, so many of them that it looked like wave upon wave crashing in from the sea, he faded into the background as if he'd never been there.

It took nearly forty stitches to close my side, and Psycho Stan needed nine months to recover from his collapsed lung. Brian lost a kidney and spent some time in jail after he recovered.

It was my first trip to Europe, and I never wanted to go back again.

NINETEEN

I STILL HAD my backstage credential, and that allowed me to hang out around Gorilla and watch Mike Austin and Scotty Prichard hold the show together. They were good, too, anticipating shots and calling for camera changes. Everything in the show was timed down to fifteen-second increments, and if one segment went long, others would have to be shortened or scrapped altogether.

A production assistant held a printed copy of the script and kept time with an old-fashioned stopwatch, feeding information to the producers when they needed it. Mostly, though, they didn't need it. Everything in the back of Malone's show ran like a well-oiled machine. His processes were so streamlined and so effective that they were essentially industry standards, and even startup companies and smaller independent shows mostly used Malone's methods to run their shows.

Chaos ruled the commercial breaks. That's when producers would update everyone, from the commentators and announcers to the agents and boys in the back, of changes. Finding a minute to cut from a promo here or a match there, or even pushing a segment off the show entirely was done entirely on the fly, entirely by feel. Writers and talent in the back had to respond to those changes and get ready to perform flawlessly on worldwide TV, and everyone who was in the next segment had to be ready to hit their mark.

Walking a tightrope over Niagara Falls might have been more physically taxing, but not by much. Austin and Scotty were bathed in sweat. Malone Tomlinson may have left the building—and maybe by then he had released the driver from the trunk of his Rolls—but Malone would obsess over a recorded version of the broadcast. Even if they nailed everything, Malone would find something to critique. Nothing was ever perfect. But Austin and Scotty knew what Malone was like. They'd worked for him for a long time.

Penny Baker stopped by to ask how I was doing.

"I've got a few minutes before I'm up," she said, her voice a smoky whisper. "Have you learned anything?"

I shook my head.

"I may know less now than when I started."

Penny put her hand on my arm, then stood on tiptoe to kiss my cheek. Her lips were very soft.

"You're a dear man, Alex. You know Ray didn't deserve your loyalty."

I took a deep breath and let it out slowly. In the course of one night, I had found out that my best friend was not who I thought he was. That he had terrorized women, that he'd allowed himself to be turned into a mule for the locker room. I was confronting Ray's past and my own complicity in it, and I didn't much care for the things that I was learning.

Penny and I stepped into a narrow, curtained-off alcove that had two advantages: We could speak more privately, and we wouldn't distract the show runners in Gorilla.

"I don't understand why you won't let this go," she said. "All you're doing is hurting the show. You're hurting yourself, too.

Maybe you're even hurting Ray. Why do you need to dig up all of this bad feeling?"

Her words were full of sympathy, and that may have been what hurt most of all. I guess every adult has been betrayed by someone they trusted, someone they loved, at one point in their lives.

"I don't know," I said. "I don't think I'm doing this for Ray anymore, Penny. I think this is for me. Maybe it sounds dumb, but I feel like I'm burying my past. Coming to terms with who Ray was, who I was."

Penny didn't say anything. She bumped my shoulder companionably with her temple.

"I don't even know who I am," I said. "I hung up the boots, but I dream about this shit every day. It got in my blood. I'm a wrestler, damn it."

"We're not wrestlers, you know that. We're personalities now. Sports entertainers." She spit the last word out like she had a mouth full of shit.

"That's showbiz, baby," we said in unison, and laughed. The phrase had been one of Malone's pet phrases for years. Inside the wrestling business, his show had been known for caring far more about the sizzle than the steak, and it showed in the in-ring product. The vignettes, interviews, and other parts of UCW's show were top notch and entertaining as hell. The in-ring product had been its weakest point, until guys like Ray had showed up.

The first time Ray heard Malone say "That's showbiz, baby," he had made fun of him to his face, roasting him so hard that Malone abruptly stopped using the phrase. Ray found it insulting. But Malone had been right. What else was pro rasslin' but old-fashioned showbiz?

It's a one-ring circus, a carnival all its own. At its best, wrestling is live, athletic theater that allows you to lose yourself in its chaotic world. And when the show comes to town, people plunk down their money to come to watch.

"You should ask Lara out," Penny said, breaking into my thoughts.

"Who?"

"You know, the one carved out of marble, perfect looks?"

"Right, the one boring a hole in me with her stare. No thanks. When I start dating again, I'd like to live through it. Besides, I'm twice her age."

"Maybe she has a thing for older men."

"Maybe she'd like to give someone a heart attack."

"What, you think it'd be the first time?"

Penny Baker was just old enough to be a mother hen to the other women on the roster. She was an old pro by then, although like any of the Queens, she would have balked at using the word 'old' to describe herself. She was experienced, wised up. Back in my day we would have said that Penny was smart to the business. She hit her time cues without fail, and she was always in the right place at the right time. Maybe even more important, I didn't know of a single time that Penny had hurt anyone in the ring. Not every wrestler speaks the phrase aloud, but the goal before a match is to leave your opponent the way you found them. No chipped teeth, no broken bones, no unplanned blood. You worked tight, and tried to make everything look good, but you also protected one another as much as possible.

Penny was one of the good ones, and she was a mother hen to the rest of the Queens, about as universally respected in the locker room as a woman could be in the boys' club of professional wrestling.

A referee I didn't know stuck his head in the little room, saw Penny, and told her she had two minutes until her segment. We hugged, and I told her to rock it out there. Penny strutted toward Gorilla, already getting into the zone where she became the person that everyone wanted to see. She flipped her hair over her shoulder and cast a glance back at me, where I was studiously not examining the way her skin-tight boy shorts fit her from the rear. She dropped a wink, turned away from me, and went toward the crowd.

I hadn't paid close attention to the run sheet, so I wasn't sure whether Penny had a match or a promo. It might have been both. Historically, women were used as special attractions at wrestling shows, with only a very few appearing on any card. That had changed in recent years, with Malone and his daughter, Melanie, building a real division for the women. Melanie didn't travel with the show anymore, preferring to stay home and raise her children. So Penny was the de facto leader of the Queens.

Why did that keep troubling me?

I found my way upstairs, knocked on the Queens' locker room door. Lara answered, and after making sure that no one was changing clothes, she let me in. I was looking for Kat, and I found her in one corner. She was seated on the floor in some approximation of a lotus position, breathing deeply, her eyes closed. I didn't waste any time with pleasantries.

"Something is bothering me, kid. I keep thinking about Penny, about how she's so protective over all of you."

Kat opened her eyes. She was an absolutely beautiful woman, but those eyes were her best feature. She could convey any emotion: pain, anger, longing, sadness, joy. The camera loved her, and she was the one Queen who was often offered small roles in large films and large roles in small films. When she looked at me now, I saw only resignation.

"Alex," she said, rising from the floor without apparent effort. "Don't ask me. I don't want to get involved."

There were two bags on the bench next to her. One of them was a standard black rolling bag. The other one was hot pink and featured stickers of anime characters that I'm sure some fanboy would recognize.

"I have to know," I said. "It wasn't you, was it?"

Kat hung her head. Around us, the women's dressing room was now empty. Most of the female talent was probably off waiting for a cue, running lines, or talking with agents about their segments. I could hear a shower somewhere behind me, but I didn't look around. It was just Kat and me, so I pressed.

"I've never asked you for anything, have I?" Kat wouldn't look at me, but I saw a tear drop from her face and splash against the floor near her feet. "I'm asking now. I don't know that we're friends, exactly, but we've always been friendly. Help me."

Kat answered in a low monotone, her voice devoid of all the life and vitality that her eyes conveyed so easily. I told her what I wanted, and Kat moved mechanically to the rolling pink suitcase with all the stickers. She unzipped the front compartment and came out with Penny's cell phone. Kat tapped in the security code and handed it to me.

One look at the mapping application on Penny's phone told me everything I knew. Kat called after me, but by then I was already halfway down the stairs, my knees reminding me that sometime after I'd retired, I'd let myself become an old man. When Penny's segment was over, I was back at Gorilla, waiting for her. When she came through the curtain, she was still pumped from the crowd, full of the euphoria of performing in front of a packed house, a high that never got old. But like any addiction, you needed more and more of it to get along in this bad old world.

She stopped smiling when she saw me. Maybe it was my face. Somewhere between leaving Kat and arriving at the staging area, I had grown cold. I don't even know that I was angry anymore. What I felt most of all was tired and sick of everything about the wrestling business. Everything seemed unreal. The colorful ring gear appeared muted, and the house music that played during commercial breaks sounded as though it were coming through wads of cotton.

A stagehand returned Penny's ring jacket to her, and she folded over her hands. She approached me, tried to touch my arm, I pulled away. Penny peered up at me through her dark, artfully teased bangs. Around us, the show went on. We ignored everything but each other.

"Let it go. Please."

"I can't do that, Penny. Ray was my friend."

She brushed past me, heading for the locker room, and I followed in her wake. Her breath hitched in her chest, and she held the sequined ring jacket against her body as if it would protect her from what she had done. As if it would protect her from me. The fine, intricate muscles in her shoulders tensed and relaxed as she walked.

Catering was deserted by this time. The last scraps of food were gone, and we were alone. Penny kept her jacket between us as if it were a shield against the truth.

"He had to be stopped, Alex. Maybe you don't believe that, and I wouldn't blame you. But nobody did anything, no matter how much we complained, no matter what we said, no matter what we did. He wouldn't stop. Maybe he couldn't."

Her eyes were shiny as she turned her face to me. Tears tracked thick mascara down her unlined cheeks, and one of her false eyelashes had begun to come loose.

"He was after Kat again, did you know that? I couldn't let that happen. I lost her to him once. I stopped him, Alex. I stopped the bastard."

Then she dropped her ring jacket, and there was a gun in her hand. She turned the pistol on me.

TWENTY

May 15, 1986
Somewhere near Lake Charles, Louisiana

ALMOST EVERY WRESTLER I ever knew carried a gun in their bag. I kept mine on the passenger seat when I drove. Just a little insurance against the marks, that's all. I had it on me every time we arrived at a building and always when we departed.

We were leaving Baton Rouge, Louisiana, one night, driving on to Houston. It's a straight line down I-10, four hours or so if you drive the speed limit, but none of the boys could keep their cars under ninety. We flew down that straightaway after the matches, beer cans propped against our crotches, hands only occasionally on the wheel.

You could theoretically fly to Houston if you wanted to, but that meant small planes and potentially bad weather blowing up from the Gulf of Mexico, and neither of those appealed to us. Ray had survived a plane crash once, early in his career, and he wasn't eager to repeat the experience. Less than four hours in a car on the Interstate was a tit for me in those days, so we rented a Mercedes 300D. Ray rode in the rear, his head tilted back and eyes closed. The only sign of life that I saw through occasional glances at the rear-view mirror was when he lifted a beer can to his lips every now and then.

The Wild Child was on fire that night, wrestling Norvell "Sly Dog" Dromo for nearly an hour. Sly Dog, maybe six-four and two hundred and ninety pounds, had carved out an unlikely main event position for himself in one of the most schizophrenic territories in the United States. Part of the territory was Louisiana and the western half of Mississippi. The other part was Arkansas and Oklahoma. Sly was a huge, powerfully built Black man, and he was about as over with the crowds in the eastern half of the territory as it was possible to be. In Little Rock and Oklahoma City, he still made the top of the card. But those deep South audiences were rabid for him.

Sly had out-of-this world charisma, and the fans in Baton Rouge and New Orleans would have killed for him if he'd asked them to. Unfortunately, he wasn't in good enough shape to work the kind of match that Ray could have. Nowadays, through the lens of whatever 'wrestling history' is, people say that all of Ray's matches were repetitive. There's some merit to that, but the truth was that Ray had streamlined his style so that he could carry anyone to a good match.

That night, Ray led Sly Dog around the ring like he was a puppy on a leash. Give Sly credit: he was there for every spot the Wild Child called. But weeks before, Ray and Brutus Feller had already come up with an angle that would get Sly out of the match without losing face.

Brutus Feller was a longtime fan favorite in the territory, what the Hollywood film people might call a second lead. He was generically handsome and a good hand in the ring. His promos were never that great, but they didn't need to be. He had enough spark in the ring during his matches that the fans always looked forward to seeing him. If Sly couldn't headline a show, Brutus could be moved up to the main event, no problem.

The storyline problem for Sly and Brutus came when the North

American championship was held up. Now, normally, Ray would come into the territory and face the reigning champion for the world title. But with the title held up, promoter Andrew Davie set up a legit voting hotline in his office, and Sly won going away, as Davie knew he would. The promoter then booked Brutus to win the North American title. Sly got the title shot against Ray, but Brutus had a legitimate complaint, because the regional champion is the one who got a chance at the big belt.

For three weeks of television, Brutus publicly backed Sly Dog, saying that he would be happy to take on the Dog for the world title after he beat Ray. Then a curious thing happened. Davie named Brutus as the referee for the world title match. The fans in Baton Rouge were ecstatic. The Wild Child had a well-established history of evading a loss to top regional talent like Sly by some technicality or other. But with the well-liked Brutus Feller as the referee, fans assumed a title change would take place.

Ray and Sly went about twenty minutes that night before going to the finish, with Brutus calling the action completely down the middle, and maybe favoring Sly Dog just a little. Sly made his big comeback, bouncing the Wild Child from pillar to post. He lifted Ray onto one massive shoulder, backed into the corner, and hit a running powerslam on Ray right in the middle of the ring.

The thing about that kind of powerslam is that it puts you into position for a pin. When Sly drove Ray down to the mat, that should have been the three count, as far as the fans were concerned. And it would have been, except that Brutus took that opportunity to leap into the air as high as he could and drive his knee directly into the head of the Sly Dog.

The Dog rolled off of Ray, who took a few seconds to gather his breath. While that was going on, Brutus Feller was beating the ever-loving shit out of Sly. Punches to the face, kicks to the groin, gouges to the eye. No one had ever seen Brutus Feller act this way before. The fans erupted. Some of them tried to rush the ring, but police kept them back.

What happened next keyed the biggest money run of Brutus Feller's life. Ray strutted over to Brutus, high-fived him, and then set Sly up for a piledriver, which was considered a potentially lethal finishing move at the time. The move appears to spike your opponent directly onto the crown of their head, and it is dangerous enough in real life that larger companies did in fact ban it for the safety of their talent. But that was years away from this night in Baton Rouge. Ray and Feller teamed up for six piledrivers in all. When they were done, Sly was a quivering mass in the center of the ring.

Ray arrogantly put one foot on Sly Dog's chest, and Brutus dropped to the mat to count the pinfall and award the match to Ray. Brutus was still supposedly the referee for the title match, and he hadn't called for the bell until Ray pinned his opponent.

It hadn't been Ray's best match, but it was a great angle that set the territory on fire for the next year, as Dog tried to get revenge on Brutus.

Ray and I had to wait until every fan had left the building and the cops cleared the parking lot before we went to the car that night.

The interstate was quiet, with few cars and only not many big trucks zipping along under the black sky. In those days you had to watch out for anything weird along the highway. The eighteen wheelers, piloted by guys cracked out of their gourds on speed or cocaine, had little regard for smaller vehicles. They had loads to pull and schedules to make. I gave them a wide berth, but kept the pedal almost all the way down to the metal for nearly two hours until Baton Rouge felt safely behind us.

We dropped off the interstate at Lake Charles, taking an exit for fuel and restrooms. When I was done pumping diesel and Ray finished blowing up the gas station toilet, we grabbed some snacks and another twelve-pack of beer. On our way out the door, we ran into some fans of Ray's, a couple of good ol' boys in sagging, ragged jeans, camo tee shirts, and John Deere trucker hats. They looked like they carried the spare tire for their vehicles around their middles, guys with suspect dental hygiene and confrontational body odor.

"Hey, ain't you that rassler?"

Now, Ray was most certainly that *rassler*. He could hardly be anything else. Ray was a little over six feet tall, with broad shoulders and narrow hips. His thick blonde hair was still partially wet from the shower, and he had a piece of athletic tape on his forehead to cover the area where he'd gigged himself earlier during the match against Sly Dog. A few drops of blood had seeped through the tape. It was past midnight, and Ray still wore gray slacks and a navy blazer with pewter buttons. His white dress shirt was spotless. He was obviously the Wild Child, Ray Wilder. But it was late and Ray didn't want to get into anything.

"No," he said, and stepped around them. The two extras from Deliverance looked at me. I shrugged and shouldered past them, too. They didn't recognize me, or if they did, they didn't say anything about it. The pair hustled after Ray as if I wasn't there. They were keyed in on him the way a pack of wild predators will fixate on one animal. Maybe it was the blood seeping through the makeshift bandage on Ray's forehead. Regardless, the two of them followed us into the parking lot with its cracked and weedy pavement. The only other vehicle there at that time of night was a jacked-up Ford F-150, its tires worn down to baloney skins. It rumbled and hitched like a living thing, and black exhaust seeped from its tailpipe like the smoke of a sleeping dragon. Neither of the corn pone cowboys had thought to shut the engine.

"Hey, come on, man. We just want to talk. We like to rassle, too. Maybe you want to rassle one of us?"

Ray already had the twelve-pack torn open by the time he reached the Mercedes. He put the beer down on the seat, got in, and shut the door. He was drinking deep from the can by the time the rednecks got there. One of them slapped the roof of the car hard enough to leave a dent.

"We'us talking to you," he shouted through the glass. Ray looked at him, dead-eyed. "Come on out, show us that title belt. Don't be a sissy, man. We wanna rassle, too."

I was maybe ten feet behind them at that point. The plastic bag full of snacks swung in my left hand. I kicked one of them in the back of the knee. It collapsed, and he staggered down to the pavement. His twin—whether genetic or simply in predisposition—whirled around, his hands up like he wanted to make something out of it.

"Hey, what the hell are you doing?"

"Let's not fuck around about this," I said. "You boys go on your way, and we'll go on ours. Nobody will get hurt, and you'll have a story to tell your buddies."

"Hey, fuck you, I think you broke my leg," the one on the ground spat through gritted teeth. "I'm gonna even that up."

"Is that right?" I asked. My voice was mild. Neither of them responded. Around us was the absence of human sound. Along the interstate, vehicles buzzed past. Somewhere in the trees, cicadas sang their mating call to one another. But here, under the blinding sodium-arc lights, there was no sound. Nothing left to say.

I walked around to the driver's side of the car. The two watched me go. I opened the door, tossed in the plastic bag, and then reached into the door pocket of the Mercedes and brought out a short-barrelled Smith & Wesson .357 Magnum revolver. Those guns were all the rage in those days, and I made sure that they saw it. I didn't point the pistol at anyone. Not then.

I stepped over to their truck and raised the gun, keeping the two morons within my line of vision.

"What are you —"

The first shot nearly deafened me, and one of the truck's rear tires exploded. The truck frame sagged to one side. I shot one of the front tires as well, and the truck seemed to settle into its new, half-tired existence with a sigh. It wasn't enough. I put a bullet through their windshield, and another through the radiator. The truck died then, with a horrible gasping sound. Steam rose from under the hood and disappeared into the night like it had never been there.

"That's four shots," I said, staring down the rednecks. "I've got two left."

I paused, as if I had just made the connection.

"Hey," I said, and smiled my widest and most genuine smile. "There are two of you."

They took off. The uninjured one reached a pretty good speed, while the one that I'd kicked had to make a limping getaway. I watched them go, then hopped back behind the steering wheel of the Mercedes.

I cranked the car and glanced back at Ray in the rear-view. His head was back. His eyes were closed. He might not have moved during all of the commotion.

"You having fun?" He asked.

"A little, yeah."

"Can we please fucking go now? There's a flight attendant in Houston who's waiting on me, and you're out here goofing off with Jack and Jerk, the Off brothers."

I shifted into Drive and we hopped back on I-10.

"Hey, Ray," I said.

"Yeah?"

"Has she got a friend?"

TWENTY-ONE

IT WAS SCOTTY who saved me. He walked into catering, speaking into the microphone on his wireless headset. He wasn't paying any attention to us, and in fact had his head down, looking at a copy of the run sheet, and he walked directly between Penny and me. His face was drawn with strain, eyes pouchy and red from like he'd sneaked away from Gorilla to take a quick smoke break. Penny fired the gun, and Scotty jerked in mid-stride. He looked at me, red eyes widening, and started to fall.

I caught him by the armpits and tried to slow his descent to the floor. An ugly red stain spread across his UCW-branded sport shirt. In that moment, I knew that I was dead, knew that Penny would turn the gun on me and that I would soon join Ray Wilder in whatever kind of afterlife there was for broken down old wrestlers like me. But I couldn't just let Scotty fall. He had no idea what he'd walked into. I didn't want to let him die alone. I had known him too long, and if we weren't close any longer, he was still my friend.

Even if he hadn't done it on purpose, Scotty had taken a bullet meant for me.

Penny stared at us, her mouth forming a huge, wet O of surprise. Scotty Prichard hadn't done anything to her. Unlike Ray, she'd had no grievance against him. She dropped the gun, flinging her hand away from it as thought she were a little girl who had touched a hot stove and been burned. The gun bounced into a corner, and I lost sight of it for a moment.

Penny stood rooted to the floor, as if she had been turned to stone by the horror of what she had done. When I caught Scotty, his weight had carried me down to the floor. It had cushioned his fall, but my knees screamed complaints about their impact with the hard concrete floor. Scotty's forehead was drenched in sweat, turning his deep rust-colored hair a darker shade of burnished copper. His headset was askew, and I could hear the chatter from the production team through one earphone. His eyes were wide and wild as he searched my face.

"Hang on," I said. "Don't talk. I got you. I got you."

I pulled the headset all the way free and placed it on my head, ignoring the fact that the cushioned earpieces were drenched in someone else's sweat.

"Can anybody hear me?" My voice came out in a loud panicked rush, and distortion filled my ears. I nearly ripped the headset off.

"Scotty, is that you? Say again. Where are you? Live shot in fifteen seconds." Mike Austin's calm, professional voice came through the earpiece, and I nearly jumped for joy.

"Scotty's down. He's been shot, Mike. We need an ambulance here now."

"Donovan?"

Scotty's eyes were huge, the red veins in the sclera seemed to pulse. I hadn't tried to find the site of the wound. It wouldn't have done any good if I had. The entire left side of his shirt was wet with blood,

"Good Christ it hurts." Scotty's voice was a harsh whisper, like wind through reeds. "Ah, fuck, I don't want those to be my last words.

I patted his shoulder.

"They won't be," I said. Then I spoke to Mike again.

"We're in catering. Get someone here, quick as you can."

Large wrestling companies often employ athletic trainers, just like major league sports teams. Almost every professional athlete has some kind of nagging injury during a season. The problem for wrestlers is that there is no off-season. For years the business operated on a 'no-show, no pay' policy. If you couldn't make your dates—in other words, if you have to call in sick or injured—you don't get paid. While that policy had gone away with written contracts and downside guarantees as the business moved into the twenty-first century, it was still ingrained in professional wrestlers: you make the next town.

Malone had taken things a step further by actually hiring a physician to travel with the show. He usually dealt with sprains and strains, the occasional broken finger or ankle. But he was there at the building, thank God, and I was happy as hell to hear Mike Austin scream for him to get his ass to catering as fast as humanly fucking possible.

The doc hustled in, a medium-tall man with graying hair and a neatly trimmed goatee. He carried a black jump bag with a big white cross stitched on the side. Athletic trainers, their gear bags strapped to their waists, accompanied him. They eased Scotty off of my lap and flat onto the floor, and I moved away. My knees cracked loudly when I stood up.

"Ambulance en route, ETA less than four minutes," Mike said in my ear, and I relayed the information to the doctor. The doc and athletic trainers all wore white rubber gloves, and their hands were coated in Scotty's blood. I was, too, of course. But I was wearing all black thanks to the change of clothes earlier, so no one could see just how much blood Scotty had lost. I wasn't sure how much it was, either, but I knew that being shot was never a good thing.

I backed to the wall, trying to take in the whole room, keeping everything in front of me, when I realized that something was wrong with the picture in front of me. Something was missing.

Penny was gone.

Outside along Reverend Abraham Woods Ave., I could hear the ambulance siren screaming. The one of the medical staff had cut away Scotty's shirt, and his pale belly looked like soured milk under the room's ugly lighting. Mike Austin came through the door, his hair askew where he'd ripped his own headset off. He saw the doc working on Scotty, then saw me against the wall. He hurried over to me, trying to smooth down his hair into something approaching its normal appearance.

"What the hell happened?"

I told him.

"Gun's over there," I added, nodding toward the corner where Penny had thrown it. I was keeping an eye on it the same way you'd keep an eye on a potentially dangerous snake if you were trapped in the same room with it.

"I just fucking saw Penny," he said.

"When she came through the curtain, yeah," I said. "That's when I confronted her."

Mike shook his head.

"No, I mean I just talked to her. She said she wasn't feeling good, you know, holding her belly like it was a woman thing. Asked if she and Kat could cut out early."

"What'd you say?"

"I said yes, you asshole. What kind of jerk do you think I am?"

Answering that question wasn't going to get me anywhere. Paramedics hit the room then, shooing Malone's medical staff away. In wrestling talk, we would have said they were making the save on Scotty. It was the second time in twenty-four hours that I'd seen the Birmingham rescue squad in action. More sirens sounded, and I knew the cops would be there soon.

"Which way did she go?"

Mike's headset was hooked onto a carabiner on one belt loop.

He unclipped it, put the contraption on his head, and spoke into the microphone. He listened for a moment, said 'Thank you,' and took the headset off again.

"We've got secure parking on the top deck next door now," he said. "Some of the old-timers still park across the street, but one of the refs is pretty sure that she parked up there."

"I gotta go," I told Mike. He put a hand on my shoulder to stop me.

"You don't," he said. "Gun's over there, right? Penny's done, man. It'll have her prints on it, she'll have—whadda they call it?—gunpowder residue on her hands. Let the cops take it from here. You can let it go."

I couldn't force myself to look at Mike, but I shook free of his hand.

"No," I said finally, and my voice was full of terrible rage. "I can't."

The street in front of the Boutwell is named for a native of Birmingham, a Black pastor who attended Morehouse College with Dr. Martin Luther King, Jr. and was one of the leading figures in Birmingham's civil rights struggles of the 1960s. Every time I moved along that street, I thought of the man it was named for, Abraham Woods, who found the bodies of the four little girls who'd been blown up during the 16th Street Baptist Church bombing.

The violence had gotten so bad that people began referring to the city as Bombingham, but good people like Woods had never given up the fight to make Birmingham a more just, more equitable, city. He had a reputation as a troublemaker, an agitator. But he—and people like him—had fought their fight and ultimately succeeded. They changed Birmingham forever.

It was only a very few steps to the parking garage. I ignored my aching knees and took those steps on the run. I couldn't wait for the elevator. That would only delay me. I went up three flights of stairs as fast as I could but when my heart started thumping and jittering in my chest, I forced myself to slow down. Three more flights. I had to remember to act my age. A mostly sedentary fifty-five-year-old man shouldn't go leaping tall buildings in a single bound. Or several bounds, for that matter.

I went up the remaining three sets of stairs much more cautiously. I didn't want anyone finding my body, dead of a heart attack, in the stairwell. By the time I reached the top level, my pulse was mostly steady, though I could still hear it pounding in my ears. I opened the door and eased out into the night air.

Out there on the roof, where very few cars were parked, you could hear the city clearly. To the south, the statue of Vulcan was lit, glowing proud and fierce in the night. Along the ridge of Red Mountain, signal towers stood, red caution lights glowing against the black night sky. Overhead, planes came in low toward Shuttlesworth International Airport.

I could see the revolving glow of emergency lights reflected against the facade of Boutwell Auditorium and hear the traffic some ninety feet below. A breeze blew steadily in from the west. Penny sat on the hood of a late-model Nissan Maxima parked along the waist-high wall that separated the parking deck from open space and gravity. She was looking out at the night sky, not seeming to pay any attention to me.

I walked quietly on the concrete. I wasn't trying to sneak up on her, but I also didn't want to chase her any farther than I had to. My heart beat hard against my chest, straining, crying for more oxygen. I breathed deeply, trying not to pant after the six flights of stairs. Maybe I should have taken the elevator after all.

When I was about ten feet away, Penny tore her eyes away from the skyline and peered at me.

"There's no point in running, is there?"

My hands flexed, relaxed, flexed again. Penny's eyes widened. She hadn't removed any of her stage makeup and looked very dramatic, with black tear tracks staining her cheeks, her jawline stark and angular. Out here in the creeping dark, with only an occasional security light to provide illumination, she looked otherworldly, a gravestone angel without its wings. I stayed silent and tried to move closer.

Penny slid off the hood of the car, putting it between us. I couldn't get to her without chasing her around the thing, and if it came down to a footrace, she was going to win every time. Even if I wasn't spaghetti-legged and panting from the run up the stairs, Penny could still outrun me. I was never what anyone would call fast.

"Don't," she said. "It's all coming down now. It's all falling apart. I'm falling apart."

She wasn't the only one. Sweat coated my face. I tried to blink it away, but that didn't work. I realized that I was shaking my left hand as though I were trying to get rid of that pins-and-needles feeling you get when your arm falls asleep. I stumbled, went down to one knee.

Now the pain was starting to crest. Fire in my left arm, an invisible fist squeezing my chest. It was hard to breathe. It felt like I'd forgotten how. All those years away from the Stairmaster, the sedentary life of a mostly respectable bartender, the pounds I'd put on but never taken off. It was all piling up on me now.

I lunged to my feet, staggered over to a late-model Hyundai. Sweat spilled from my brow to the concrete floor of the parking deck roof. Penny had retreated to the retaining wall. She was watching me, her face a mask of deep concern. I knew the concern was real. But she was also a wild animal, cornered. She would do anything to get away, just like I would do anything to get my hands on her.

For years, I had been Ray's right hand. Friend, wingman, driver, lackey. He had called me his muscle, his enforcer. I had taken that role seriously. I had lived the gimmick. For more than twenty years, being Ray's best friend was all the identity I'd ever allowed myself to have. The last thing I could ever do for him was to find his killer and avenge his murder. The search itself had led me to hard truths about Ray and about myself, truths I didn't want to face. And now that I'd found his murderer, I discovered that I no longer cared.

Austin had been right. Penny was done. There'd be physical evidence and GPS data, enough to arrest her and bring her to trial, potentially even convict her. Maybe the things that Ray had done to her and the other Queens would net her a lighter sentence or let her walk scot-free. Revenge was what I'd come for, but maybe justice would be enough.

I clutched my left arm against my side as tightly as I could. It seemed to help ease the pain a bit. The world at the edge of my vision was graying a little, coming unraveled like a loose thread in a sock. I hung my head. It was too heavy to lift. I slithered down the side of the Hyundai until my ass hit the floor. The distance from sitting to lying down was too short, and I found myself looking up into the night sky and watching clouds roll slowly past a nearly full moon.

Somewhere I could hear pounding footsteps, or maybe it was just the sound of blood hammering in my ears. My breath seemed far away, my heartbeat a mere suggestion.

Later on, the investigating officers told me that I couldn't have seen the things I did. That there was no way I could have known exactly what happened on that roof. But no one has ever argued over what I saw. No one has ever said that I was substantially wrong. I've spent a lot of time thinking about it, and the best I can figure it is that I died a few moments before those cops hit the roof.

Penny didn't try to hide. She was unarmed by that point, the gun she'd used on Ray and Scotty cast aside back in the catering area. Instead, she climbed up on the retaining wall to the roof of the parking deck. The cops advanced on her, guns drawn, their shouts to get down, to stop, falling on deaf ears. One of the officers in the rear of their formation found my mostly-dead body and began CPR.

Penny walked and twirled along the concrete barrier that

separated the parking deck from open air like a tightrope walker. The wall was maybe six inches thick, and her small feet moved in dainty steps along it. She traversed the length of the wall once, and then did it again, her arms held straight out from her sides to maintain her balance.

I don't know when she decided to jump. At first I thought Penny was just being dramatic, that she would let the cops drag her down once they got close enough. But that's not what happened. Penny spun toward the street, put her feet together like a diver going off a high diving board, and leaped before anyone could reach her. Ninety-plus feet from the sidewalk, she might have lived if she'd landed any other way, but Penny dropped from the retaining wall in a swan dive. The gray and ugly sidewalk below rushed to meet her like a long-lost lover, and she went for it headfirst.

TWENTY-TWO

May 17, 1989
The Sportsplex
Dallas, Texas

IT WAS ALL coming apart, and it had been that way as long as Rafe Van Allen could remember. Rafe was Walter Van Allen's middle child, and he had wished forever that he could be like any other middle child in almost any other family: forgotten, overlooked. Always there, but mostly invisible.

Whatever retarded God there was made sure that didn't happen. Rafe would've stood out anywhere. Six-four with dark brown hair and a chiseled jawline and deeply dimpled chin, he was also an extremely talented athlete. He was a Texas state champion in the 100-meter hurdles and the javelin throw, and he'd been named to the All-Metro football team by The Dallas Morning News. It didn't matter that his grades were shit, because he had athletic scholarship offers from five different colleges just waiting for him.

But Walter Van Allen wouldn't hear of Rafe going off to college. In a family that ran to tall, athletic boys, Walter pushed each of his kids into the wrestling business, styling the promotion he owned—Classic Championship Wrestling—as the Van Allen Dynasty. He pushed his first-born son, Randall, into the business when Randall was only seventeen, a high school senior who ran to the ring to help save his father from a bloody beatdown.

Randall was the one most like Walter. He had what the old-timers called "a mind for the business," and that was a good thing, because he didn't have the body for it. At six-nine, Randall was painfully skinny and awkward to watch in the ring. But even though Dallas was a small territory—Walter usually kept only twelve to fourteen workers on the roster—it meant big money if a guy could feud with the Van Allen boys, so no one minded selling for Randall or putting him over in their matches.

Robert was next. If Rafe had the combination of athleticism and good-looks to be a real star, Robert was the best pure athlete of the bunch. He was also the one that most marched to the beat of his own drum. Where Randall was a perennial fixture at the top of the card, Robert didn't mind working the mid-card matches with top talent, losing to them in order to get them ready for big money feuds with Randall. The Van Allen boys, with their youth, charisma, and country-boy good looks, packed fans into the Sportsplex.

When Rafe turned pro, it seemed like everything was going to Walter Van Allen's plan. But that was just how it appeared from the outside. Under the radar, cracks were beginning to show. These were kids in their early twenties or late teens. Sometimes they'd show up bombed out of their gourds on booze or pills or something stronger. Ray and Randall once wrestled a TV match that was so bad that the commentary team had to explain it away to the audience, claiming that Randall had the flu and a hundred-and-two temperature, but he didn't want to disappoint his fans.

Three months after that match, Randall Van Allen went to Japan for what was supposed to be a two-week tour for big money. Eight matches in fourteen days, which was an easy schedule compared to the American territories at the time. But something went wrong. Randall never showed up for any of his matches. He was found dead in his hotel room a day later.

No one knows what killed Randall, but his drug use was an open secret in the locker room. The only rule was that you didn't tell Walter, no matter what. Walter couldn't hear a thing like that about his boys. Rumors flew: a Japanese official found Randall's body and flushed a quantity of drugs down the toilet before calling the cops; auto-asphyxiation gone wrong; a geisha fucked him to death.

In the end, the official cause of death was labeled acute enteritis. Anyone who knew the boys just kind of rolled their eyes at that and went on about their business.

Interestingly enough, the death of Randall brought about the biggest increase in Walter's business. Robert and Rafe were pushed to the forefront of the chase for Ray's world title, with the dirt sheets and glossy mags proclaiming that the Van Allen boys were the heirs apparent for the belt.

"I think about my brother all the time," Robert told a TV interviewer. "It broke my heart when he died, and I swear that I can hear him calling me. But I've got something to do before I join him. I'm gonna beat the Wild Child for that world title if it's the last thing I ever do."

In reality, it was Rafe who won the world title from Ray at a memorial show in the Astrodome, pinning the Wild Child with a backslide. The sixty thousand in attendance blew the roof off of the place in a way that the Astros had never managed to do. Even Ray, who looked at everything that happened in the ring as just business, shed tears. There's an iconic photograph out there, shot moments after Rafe's pinfall victory, where Ray and Rafe are reaching out to one another across the canvas mat, their hands clasped tightly in a sign of respect.

Rafe is openly crying in the photo, while Ray has his face buried in his other arm to hide his tears.

Three weeks later, Ray took the title back. No matter how much Walter loved and protected his boys in the Dallas office, Rafe couldn't handle the pressures of being world champion.

He showed up high to two of his title defenses, and no-showed another. Everyone in wrestling felt bad for the Van Allens, but no one was going to leave money on the table just for sympathy.

Robert took time away from wrestling, trying and failing to get clean. Rafe kept going, kept chasing highs in the ring and outside of it until one night when he drove his motorcycle through an intersection and collided with a loaded ambulance. The patient in the ambulance died, and since Rafe wasn't wearing a helmet, his perfect face took the brunt of the impact.

It broke his orbital bone, broke his nose, destroyed his teeth, broke his jaw in two places, and cost him an eye. He was lucky to be alive. He'd been charged with manslaughter after the ambulance patient died, as well as DWI. The cops found a large quantity of cocaine in one of the motorcycle's saddlebags, too. The Dallas County prosecutor gave the Van Allens a deal after Walter intervened. After multiple surgeries, Rafe did two years in a minimum security prison. Upon his release, Rafe returned to the wrestling ring. Now he wore a mask in the ring to hide his disfigurement. Young women still flocked to the matches for a while, but they no longer saw the young, good-looking stud. Now their faces were full of pity.

Walter had hoped that prison would force Rafe to clean up his act. Instead, Rafe came out of the joint with all of his old habits still full in force, and a couple of others besides. When the news broke that a former inmate had inked a tell-all book about his intimate prison love affair with a nationally recognized pro wrestler, it was too much for Rafe.

Ray and I were in town for what was being billed as Rafe's "last chance" at the world title. Most of the time in wrestling, a "last chance" means very little. There are always ways to put a guy back into the main event or into a title match. But it was Walter's way of trying to force his middle son to finally face his demons. He wanted Rafe to clean up, and the message was that he was out of the main events—and out of the big paydays—until he did so.

Rafe went to Walter's office in the Dallas Sportsplex, found his father's gun, and went downstairs to the locker room.

Ray and I were the first ones to the building that night, as we were most of the time when I was driving. We found the body and covered it with tarp so that no one had to see it. I called the cops while Ray reached out to Walter. It was a pretty cut-and-dried suicide, but the police stayed deep into the night.

You would've thought that Walter would cancel the show. Instead, the card went on as planned, with Robert—shaking and sobbing and looking like a ghost—taking Rafe's place in the main event against Ray. The fans in attendance had no idea that yet another of their hometown heroes was dead.

TWENTY-THREE

THERE'S NOTHING WRONG with a cemetery, except that it's full of dead people. Six weeks after Ray and Penny died, I was finally able to travel. I made the trip from Birmingham to Griffin, Georgia. I wasn't too long out of quadruple-bypass surgery, so I took it easy on the road. I felt like an old man, compression socks and puffy diaper-like underwear beneath my track pants. The scar on my chest was still raw and new-looking, the skin pink and puckered where the surgeon had finally removed the stitches.

Katherine Ash met me at the gate. I hauled myself out of the car, balanced my weight precariously against the blackthorn walking stick Mike Austin had sent me while I was laid up in the hospital, recovering. She was dressed in a medium-length dark gray dress. Her hair was pulled back in a simple, high ponytail, and her freshly scrubbed face was devoid of makeup. No black for her. She'd already done some mourning. Kat hugged me gently, aware of what my body had gone through on the roof of that parking garage, and of everything that had come after, too.

She held me at arms' length, looking me up and down. Her eyes were huge and full of concern.

"You've lost weight."

"Well," I said, and my voice still sounded raspy and weak in my ears, "I had a good bit to lose."

"And the cane?"

"Insurance," I said. "I get tired easier than I used to."

I used the blackthorn stick with one hand and Kat held my other elbow as we made our way to the tombstone. It was mid-morning, and the thick, well-manicured grass was still damp with dew. The sun was out, casting a bloodless heat that made very little difference in the temperature. Every few steps, I paused to enjoy the light on my face, the breath flowing easily in my lungs. We made very little sound as we walked. Kat gazed at the ground but kept her grief to herself.

We arrived at the tombstone. That's all it was. Penny Ann Baker carved in a cold marble slab. Dates of birth and death were chiseled in smaller lettering underneath her name. I didn't say anything. I couldn't. The feeling welled up in me, and I wanted to weep. I'd imagined standing here in front of Penny's marker for the entire trip over, thought of so many things I would like to say to her. But now that I was here, those words fled like cowards before battle.

Kat squeezed my arm.

"I know," she said. "I know."

"I'm sorry I couldn't be here for the service."

"Don't be silly. We spread some of her ashes around Buck Creek, down in Milledgeville, where she grew up. I put the rest in an urn."

Kat kept hold of my arm. I was glad she was there. It was good to feel a human touch after everything that happened.

"She didn't have to do it," I said. "Any of it."

Around us, everything remained quiet and muted. Even the thin and faltering sun hid its face behind a bank of gray, puffy clouds.

"I feel like it was my fault," Kat said. "She thought that Ray and

I were, you know, on again. We weren't. I'm not going to make excuses for him. He was what he was —"

"He was an asshole."

Kat smiled ruefully.

"He was," she said. "But that's not all he was, you know? If that was all he was, you would have never been friends with him. You would've never tried to look for his killer."

I craned my neck around, felt the movement pull at the still-puckered flesh on my chest.

"Yeah. And look where that got us. Two people dead. Scotty was shot. It's a goddamn mess."

"I know," Kat said. "I know. I guess I'm just looking for some kind of positive to come out of this."

I stared down at Penny's gravestone. I couldn't feel any anger, righteous or otherwise. A woman had finally gotten fed up with Ray's behavior and stopped it. I understood why she did it, even if I couldn't condone what she had done. Ever since I woke up in the hospital and they told me that I wasn't going to die—not right then, anyway—I had felt so alone and cut off from everything and everyone I knew. I wondered if that was how Penny had felt there at the end.

I hadn't brought any flowers, but now I found myself wishing that I had. I would have liked to lay them against Penny's marker and tell her that I understood.

"I had a lot of time to think about it in the hospital," I said. "I don't blame her for what she did. I can't forgive her. Not yet, anyway. But maybe I'll get there eventually."

Kat nudged me with her shoulder. We looked at each other. Her face was shiny and wet with tears.

"It's my fault, you know. She didn't start getting bad—not like she was at the end, anyway—until after I went off with Ray that time."

I put my arm around her and squeezed, just a brotherly hug.

"You can't blame yourself," I said. "Just like I can't blame myself for what Ray became. The person I discovered wasn't the man I knew. It wasn't my fault, just like the whole thing with Penny wasn't your fault."

Kat sniffled and wiped her nose.

"I could have told somebody. I could have told you."

There was nothing for me down that road. I leaned a little heavier on the walking stick.

"You told me when it mattered," I said. "You didn't have to let me see her phone. You stepped up, kid."

Kat barked a little laugh.

"You're the only person who can get away with calling me kid."

Business had gone on as usual for Malone Tomlinson and the traveling variety show he called Unlimited Championship Wrestling. The news of Ray's death generated huge numbers, as well as the revelation that Penny had killed him and then herself. Marcus Digger was all over TV, telling everyone who would listen that Ray was his idol and mentor, and that he'd been incredibly tight with Penny, too. No, he said every time he was asked, he had no idea what kind of beef the two had behind-the-scenes. Digger was quiet, introspective, and respectful in those interviews, his charm and charisma oozing from the screen. They say when you can fake sincerity, you can do anything. I thought Digger was about to rocket to superstardom. Malone wouldn't be able to keep him under contract if he could act that well.

I saw Digger in person a couple of times during my hospital stay, with the pancake makeup rubbed free of his face, and I can't say that I was disappointed to see the marks from the beating I'd given him.

I never said anything while I stood staring at Penny's marker. What would have been the point? Would she have heard me anyway? If I could understand—at least in theory—what she'd done to Ray, I still couldn't bring myself to understand the rest. Sometimes at night, when the black dog of my own depression howls and growls the loudest, I get close. I think.

Maybe Penny had looked deep enough into herself that she found someone or something that she truly couldn't live with. In my mind's eye, I can still see her walking the tightrope of that retaining wall. In memory, it seems that her mind was never made up until that last moment, when she jumped. Did she regret it?

I wish I knew.

I reached forward and touched the tombstone, fingers caressing the smooth marble. What was it that Bunny Fitzgerald had said? The Moving Finger writes; and having writ, moves on ... or something like that. Penny was gone. So was Ray. In many ways, they had it easier. People like Kat and me had to stick around and pick up the pieces.

"Have you visited Ray yet?" Kat asked.

I shook my head.

"Not going to," I said. "The guy who died at my bar wasn't the man I knew. He wasn't anyone I would even want to know."

We stood for a long time, thinking our private thoughts about Penny. She'd meant more to Kat than me, but Penny had been someone I cared for more deeply than I realized, and my respect for her hadn't diminished. In fact, it may have grown.

Finally, I turned away, thumping my way back to the car and leaning more and more of my weight on the cane as I went. It seemed a long way to drive without much effect. Kat followed me and helped me slide behind the wheel, even though I told her it wasn't necessary. I closed the door and then cranked the window down. Kat bent and laid her forearms on the opening, resting her chin atop them.

"Hey," she said, "I almost forgot. Penny said that she was going to tell you to ask Lara out. Did she ever do that?"

I grunted. She had, right before she went out for what would be her final TV segment. Kat looked through her purse for a moment, then pulled out a white card. It had Lara's name on it, and a number with a 615 area code. Nashville, maybe? I raised my eyebrows. That wasn't too far from Birmingham, I supposed.

Straight north on I-65, an easy three hours. Maybe less if I ever felt like my old self again.

"Call her sometime."

"You really think I should, even after all of this? You know I'm too old for her."

I was thinking about those stitches so recently pulled out of my chest, that traitor heart that tried to stop beating, and the deep and dark tunnel awaiting me. Lara looked like the kind of woman who would kill a healthy man, so calling her felt like digging another foot deeper into my own grave.

Kat gave me one of her patented Katherine-the-Great looks that communicated layered, sincere feeling without ever saying a word. I heard her loud and clear. She was saying that I was a damned fool if I didn't. I put the card with Lara's number on my dashboard and read it again. Maybe I'd call her after all.

After all, what else did I have to lose?

ACKNOWLEDGMENT

I GREW UP as a fan of old-school professional wrestling. My father and I spent many, many Saturdays watching the stars of Ron Fuller's Southeastern/Continental territory on TV and occasionally going to the matches in nearby Dothan. One of the difficult things when writing about wrestling is to show how wild things actually were back in the territory days. I've fictionalized several events, but the stuff that really happened back then would make the hair stand up on the back of your neck. A huge thank you to Hector Acosta, whose book Hardway (also from Shotgun Honey) paved the way for Living the Gimmick by showing me that in writing about wrestling, I could find things to say that were universal. Many thanks to my friends and fellow writers, Emily Guy Birken, James D.F. Hannah, Libby Cudmore, and Mark Westmoreland for their ideas, insightful readings, and encouragement. Having writer friends means that someone cheers you on during the hard times, and that's far more important than most people realize.

Thank you to Shaun Burnett, who is sometimes known as Scott Reznor, for being a great tag-team partner in the announcers' booth with me for several wrestling promotions and for cracking up with me at all of my terrible jokes. Thanks to the squad that includes Joe Crowe and Sarah Shierling for late-night Waffle House and other shenanigans with Shaun and me. I love you guys.

I have been inspired by a long line of writers like Donald Westlake, Robert B. Parker, Elmore Leonard, and Lawrence Block. If some of this work feels like an old friend, it's because I wrote the book in homage to them. Thank you to Ron Phillips, who believed in my work and offered me the chance to show it to the wider world. Thank you to Beth Whalen, who has known me 20 years and has always believed in my talent. And, of course, thank you to my wife, Misty, who does so much stuff behind the scenes that allows me to "be a writer."

BOBBY MATHEWS is the author of the novels *Living the Gimmick* (May 2022) and *Magic City Blues* (March 2023) from Shotgun Honey Books. He is the co-editor of the anthology *Dirty South: High Crimes & Low Lives Below the Mason-Dixon Line*, forthcoming in May 2023 from Down & Out Books. Bobby was a finalist for the 2021 Derringer Award for his story 'Quitman County Ambush.' He lives in Birmingham, Alabama, and when he's not writing fiction, he's covering sports in suburban Birmingham.

In addition to reporting and writing, he has been involved in the wrestling business on some level for several years, working as an on-camera talent and also helping book angles in promotions in Alabama and northwest Florida. Most recently, he was the lead commentator for Spartan Pro Wrestling's TV program based in Gadsden, Alabama.

He's a fan of *Jason Isbell and the 400 Unit*, *The Drive-By Truckers*, Robert Earl Keen, and anyone who sings those old, low-down, lonesome country blues. His favorite writers include Donald Westlake, Elmore Leonard, Lawrence Block, and Robert B. Parker. He lives in suburban Birmingham, Alabama--which truly is the Magic City in more ways than one--with his wife and two sons.

THANK YOU
FOR READING

LIVING THE GIMMICK
BY BOBBY MATHEWS

ENJOY THIS
SPECIAL PREVIEW OF
MAGIC CITY
BLUES

FEBRUARY 2023

ONE

ON THE BIG screen above the bar, two teams were playing for the World Cup, and I'm sure somebody somewhere cared about it.

Not me. I was drinking a cold bottle of Carta Blanca and listening to the pair next to me. Their heads were close together, but they'd had a couple and were talking the way nearly drunk people do—just a little too loud—and they were much more interesting than the TV.

"Man, I still can't believe she threw you out like that," the guy nearest me said. "I hate to hear it."

"Yeah," his friend said. "I mean, I guess I knew it would come sometime. She thought we was in a relationship; I thought we's just fucking."

And now they're neither, I thought. But you keep your nose out of other people's business, right? Things are tough all over. My bottle was empty, so I gestured at the bartender for another. The beer was going down smooth and cold, and the bar was mostly dark except for the overheads that glinted off the glassware hanging from racks mounted to the ceiling. And the TV, of course.

Neither one of them was what you'd call big. The one farther away from me—the one who'd thought that he and his woman were just fucking—was what you'd call wiry. Not six feet tall, but the cords in his forearms stood out every time he moved to lift his glass.

They were drinking gin martinis with not very much Vermouth, and I could smell the alcohol from where I sat three stools down. It was the middle of the afternoon and they were tipsy going on drunk. I looked at my beer. Most of it was gone. If I wasn't careful, I'd get tipsy, too.

But I had things I needed to do, work that couldn't wait much longer. Maybe I'd made a mistake with the beer. There was some pressure south of my belt buckle, and I remembered that old saying: you never really buy beer, just rent it for a little while. I stayed put. Of course I did. Being patient is part of the job, and I pride myself on being professional. When the one nearest me shoved away from the bartop and said, "I gotta break the seal," I slid from my own stool and managed to stumble into him when he tried to pass.

"Oh, hey," he said as he grabbed my arm to keep me from falling. "You all right old-timer?" I didn't say anything. I couldn't. While he was helping me stand, I put my hands on him, too. A quick dip into his pockets, a nudge to the ankle with the side of my foot.

No gun.

That was good. I don't carry on jobs like this one, not since I got arrested and my attorney had to do a little fancy footwork to keep me out of jail on a weapons charge about five years ago. But I still worked all the time around people who carried a gun, and it made me cautious when I wasn't carrying one.

He headed to the men's room and I followed about two steps behind him, giving him just enough space to step through the door before I came through like a freight train. I had my fist tight against my shoulder and I drove the point of my elbow horizontally into the base of his skull.

He stumbled forward, tried to catch himself on the white porcelain sink. But it was slippery with water and his hands skidded along the smooth slick surface. I got a right hook into his kidney and he kind of slumped down, an agonized chuff of wind exploding from his mouth. I caught a glimpse of myself in the mirror and didn't recognize the man looking back at me. There were two bright, hard red spots high on my cheekbones, right underneath my eyes, but other than that my face was as pale and emotionless as death itself.

I got one hand under his collar and turned him around to face me, slapping one rough palm over his mouth before he could scream. His eyes were wide and sweat trickled down his forehead. His hands were locked on my forearm and he made little mewling sounds against my palm.

"I don't know if you're wearing a wire," I whispered, spitting the words like venom from a snake's mouth. "I don't care, either. We have a mutual friend. He'd like you to shut your piehole. If you don't do it yourself, he's gonna send me around again, and we'll have to work out a more permanent solution. Nod if you understand."

He nodded. Snot trickled out of his nose and onto my hand. I let him go and punched him. Just the belly. My orders were clear: Leave no marks on his face. So I pounded his ribs with a couple of shots, and when he turned away, bent over and clutching his abdomen, I aimed a kick right between his legs, getting up under him hard, doing my best to punt him like a football. That was the closest he came to screaming, but there wasn't enough air left in his body to actually make the sound. Instead his mouth was drawn out in a silent rictus of pain.

It wasn't enough.

While he knelt puking on the floor, I stepped on his ankle with my thick-soled shoes and heard a bone crack.

I washed my face at the sink and used the paper towel on the bathroom door handle. If the cops wanted to, they could get my prints from either of the bottles I'd used. But I was betting there wouldn't be any cops. I opened the door and walked out. The afternoon sun glaring into the bar looked a few shades darker. I left a couple of bills on the bar to pay my tab, and then I walked past Mr. I-Thought-We's-Just-Fucking and out the door. It was summer, so the sunlight was still strong, even though it had dropped deep into the western sky.

I walked a couple of blocks to a little pocket park over on 76th Street, where I sat down on a green iron bench and texted the client. Message delivered. Only time would tell if the message was received.

I'm muscle for hire. You need someone protected? I can do it. Somebody owes you and doesn't pay? I can collect. And sometimes I run a messenger service, like today. Better than a certified letter. My messages tend to stay with people, even after they get out of the hospital.

I put the phone back in my pocket. Sat on the bench and watched the world come back into focus. It was deep in summer, and the green world around me was abuzz with bees and butterflies. Somewhere nearby a woodpecker hammered percussion in a band no one else could hear. Nature red in tooth and claw.

The phone buzzed, a notification of payment sent to an app, which would eventually be electronically transferred to my bank. All clean and tidy. It made me think of the early days on the street, scrapping. Poor white boy, no money in his pockets, would fight anybody over anything, without the slightest provocation. Of course, I still didn't have any money in my pockets. Money doesn't mean what it used to. It's no longer a wad of cash concealed in a handshake once the job is done. Now it's electronic transfers, all ones and zeroes. I don't understand it. All I know is that I still don't have any cash in my pockets.

The platinum card in my wallet isn't bad, though.

That was the year I was living in the Sky Inn, a not-quite-condemned pile of cinderblocks, shingles, and roach-infested carpet on the 6000 block of First Ave. on the east side of Birmingham. Yeah, I could've lived somewhere nicer if I'd wanted to, but the place had its charms. Each room came with its own drug dealer. And in that neighborhood, no one gave a damn about my comings and goings. Gunshots and knifings and clubbings went unremarked and unreported. My neighbors tended to be like me: gentrified right out of the Crestwood and Avondale neighborhoods, looking for a permanent place to light. I rented by the week, a hundred bucks due every Sunday before noon.

I was sitting in the glowering darkness of my room early on a Monday afternoon, staring at the gray blank screen of the broken TV when Carlton Doyle called me.

I carry the standard twenty-first century communications device, a small black flat rectangle that makes me feel dumber every time I look at it. I don't spend a lot of time on it, but it's got the usual slew of social media apps, something that told me the weather, and everything I needed for online banking. It tracked every incoming and outgoing call. Somewhere in a data center in Bumblefuck, Nebraska, there would have been a record of Carlton's call.

But he went through the motel switchboard instead. There's a reason he runs most of the organized crime in the greater Birmingham area. He ain't dumb.

When the phone rang, I gave it the surprised and ultimately suspicious look that most of us living in this new century use. We don't talk on the phone anymore. Texts and instant messages — in an emergency, emails — are the way we reach out and touch someone these days. But since I'd grown up before all that, I still remembered how to answer the phone.

"Hello?" I said. My voice sounded rusty, like something long unused.

"Do you know who this is?"

I didn't have to lie. I'd been in Doyle's presence four or five times over the years, fixing problems he needed solved.

"Yes."

"My office. One hour."

The line went dead. Self-assured prick. Maybe I didn't want to go to his office. Maybe I had big plans, sit here in my room and watch the gray TV screen while the window-unit air conditioner droned in the background.

I took a quick shower and shaved carefully. In the alcove that passed for a closet, three suits hung. I took the best one down, a charcoal gray number with narrow blue pinstripes, and paired it with a shirt that nearly matched the color of the pinstripes. I put on gray socks and a pair of black tasseled loafers that needed a shine. I theaded a black belt through the loops of the pants and put a spring-clip holster at the small of my back. An Airweight .38-caliber revolver went into it. It's a little hammerless number, easily concealed. I figured it would be perfect for a trip to downtown Birmingham. If I ever decided to go on safari, I had a .357 Magnum that doubled as an elephant gun locked in the portable safe beneath the hotel room bed.

I tried not to think about the differences between the message I'd delivered the day before and my appointment with Doyle, but it was impossible to ignore. Even under the best of circumstances, Carlton Doyle was dangerous.

I spent a few minutes debating what kind of tie to wear, but finally decided the hell with it. On an hour's notice, Doyle probably didn't care what I looked like when I got to his place.

That was one of the differences between us. I cared. It ain't just what you do; it's how you look while you're doing it.

I heard that from a Boston P.I. one time, and I've never forgotten it.

The drive downtown was a reminder that I wasn't from Birmingham, I just lived there. People who knew the city, who lived with it and made up its beating heart, knew the surface streets much better than I did. That's why I always took the interstate, much to my chagrin. It wasn't any faster, with orange cones blocking some exits and guiding the off-ramps to others. The Department of Transportation was still hell-bent on fucking up traffic in central Alabama for the foreseeable future, and was doing a fine job of it. I got off before Malfunction Junction and found the John Hand building right where it was supposed to be, at the corner of 20th and Second Ave.

A private elevator took me to the eighteenth floor, where a bubbly blonde receptionist took my card, looked at the name discreetly, and told me that Mr. Doyle would be right with me. I'd seen the secretary a few times before. Maybe one day she'd remember my name.

I took a seat on a white leather settee that looked more expensive than the entire motel I lived in and checked my appearance in the mirror. The suit fit well, even though I'd lost some pounds — or maybe because I had — but my sandy blond hair needed a cut. My teeth were white and mostly even, but the lines in my face were etched deep by sorrow or time or both. I'll never look forty again. My complexion was too pale, the color of skin that doesn't see a lot of daylight.

Doyle's reception area was tony, with a lot of gold leaf and real plants, the kind that needed to be watered regularly. There was an old-fashioned water cooler that advertised Poland Springs water. I could get a cupful and sit back on the sofa with it. Have something to do with my hands.

On the receptionist's desk, a discreet chime sounded. She looked down once, and then back up to me. Her smile was brilliant and charming and devoid of any independent human warmth.

"Mr. Doyle will see you now."

She dropped her gaze without a second's hesitation. So much for the good suit. Maybe if I'd worn the tie. I went past her desk — I knew the way — and opened a frosted glass door.

SHOTGUN HONEY

2012 • 2022

CELEBRATING 10 YEARS OF

FICTION WITH A KICK

THE ROAD IS JUST BEGINNING

shotgunhoneybooks.com

CPSIA information can be obtained
at www.ICGtesting.com
Printed in the USA
LVHW090947140622
721240LV00012B/187

9 781956 957075